Broken, But Not Destroyed

By Tori Kane

First off, I would like to give the honor to God and thank him personally for allowing me the opportunity to share my talent so the world could see that all things are possibly through him. I would like to dedicate this book to all those people who played a part in making me into the grown beautiful successful African American woman I am today. Without any of you there would be no me and I humbly would like to thank each one of you guys from the bottom of my heart. For you guys seen something in me that it took a while for me to see and through it all y'all never turned your backs on me and stayed loyal to me in every way. I was blessed to have such people placed in my life and I am forever grateful to have been able to share time with you all over the years. I don't need to name any of you because at the end of every day you all know who you are, and with that being said I love each and every one of you and I pray God is forever blessing you as you continue to live your lives. Thank you

1

  Karly remembered it as if it were just yesterday, sitting at the table in her grandmother's house looking out the window wondering how it would feel to be grown, and as free as a bird. She was a little short to be her age with a caramel skin tone and bright brown eyes with an oval shaped face. It was just another summer day around all her cousins doing things cousins do while being home for summer break. There was a total of nine children who lived there and five adults at the time. The adults were all at work as her and her cousins ripped and ran all up and through the house, while being careful not to mess up their grandmother's antiques she had sitting in a glass covered shelf. Back then it was nice to dream of being an adult without a worry in the world. You see this was back in the days when kids would get their behinds handed to them when they stepped out of line doing anything they weren't supposed to do.

 One day Karly along with her cousins Mike, David, Alex, Jane, Melissa, as well as her little sister Alice were outside playing when another group of kids came to their neighborhood to start trouble with them. Now Mike was the oldest of them all and was the one left to keep an eye on all the rest of them, however he was always glued to the television in their grandmother's room, so he never knew what they were all outside doing. Mike was dark skin with light hazel eyes and a slim build who played third baseman on the little league team in their city. David was Mike's younger brother, and he was brown skin with a head shaped like a peanut on the top who cussed really bad and didn't care who told when he cussed. As the kids who weren't from their neighborhood started to throw cucumbers at them from the field across from where Karly's grandma lived. David went to tell Mike what

2

was going on while Karly and the rest of her cousins tried hard to resist joining in to throw cucumbers back at the kids when out of the peer blue sky a cucumber had hit one of the cousins and everybody started to engage into what you would call a cucumber fight.

Well into the fight one of the neighborhood adults who knew that Karly and her cousins didn't belong out the house and rushed to the factory where their grandma worked to inform her of what was going on. That day ended with everyone being spanked and sent to bed early for being disobedient and not listening to what the adults of the house had told them. As time passed and all the kids grew up, they started to branch off and have their own set of friends, however they still all lived in the same house so they still enjoyed one another's company in the evening. It was now later that year, and the Holiday season was approaching so everyone would be on their best behavior so that they would get exactly what they asked for that Christmas. However, what the family didn't know was this Christmas was going to be the beginning of a new chapter in all their lives and nobody was ready for it.

It was a cold winter night and all the children in the house were getting ready for bed as their grandma came into the room to tell them all goodnight and not to forget to say their prayers. They all shouted out "OK MOMMOM" which is what they called her, and she shut the door and went on about her night. Mike, David, Alex, Jane, Melissa, Alice and Karly all began to talk softly as they started to dose off one by one until they all were fast asleep. When morning came, they noticed there was no smell of breakfast being cooked as normal on Saturday mornings. Karly along with all her cousin headed out into the living room to watch cartoons on the television as they wait for an adult to go in the kitchen to prepare breakfast. Karly looked outside and noticed her Uncle Chris was out there doing something in the yard over by the water pump, so she didn't bother to ask him what was for breakfast. Uncle Chris was about 6 feet tall with glasses and a slim figure who dressed like a pimp every day. He had been born with a skin disease, so he had spot in his complexion but overall, he was brown skin. As all the children continued to watch cartoons Jane took Karly's doll from her causing her to cry and run in the room to her grandma to snitch on Jane. Jane had a caramel complexion with brown eyes, a big forehead and two front teeth missing. She noticed her grandma was still asleep but not in her bed, she was face down on the floor. Karly and Jane knew she normally slept on her bed but being only six and eight years of age they really didn't think much of it. Soon the two of them had went back to watching cartoons with the rest of the cousins only to start fighting on one another again and both ending up back in their grandma's room where she was still laid face down on the floor. This time Mike who was the oldest child in the house went out on the steps to tell his dad which was Karly's Uncle Chris, who then came in the house and told his sister Shauntae to call 911 so they could get their mother some help.

    As Karly's aunt was on the phone calling her other siblings telling them something had happened to their mother the ambulance arrived. Karly always wondered how her aunt Shawntae could dial any number on the phone because she had fingernails that curled up on both her hands, but she managed that day. Aunt Shawntae was very tall and had a very light skinned complexion and just about all the

4

men around the neighborhood had crushes on her. The paramedics walked in the house, and it was a house with no steps so when the paramedic started to ask Shauntae if her mother fell down the steps, it offended her, and she went into psycho mode. At this moment all the children in the house were scared and confused because the woman they "mom mom" was being wheeled out on what they called a bed. This was the last time they would ever see their grandma in that house again. Days went by and Karly along with all her cousins would ask when their mom mom would be returning. Karly believed her cousin Alex who was a fat short brown skin little boy was only starting to whine about their grandma because whenever he was scared of something his grandma would fix him two jelly sandwiches and he believed that would get rid of everything bad that came his way.

 The answer they would always get was when she is feeling better, she will be back home, in which Karly and her cousins would set down quietly as the adults would go into another part of the house and talk about the situation that they could be getting ready to face. None of the adults wanted to think about the fact that their mother may be ready to leave them for good. Of course, they had been through losing their father several years before any of them had children except one of them who actually had one child at the time of their father's passing, however the thought of losing their mother was way more intense because they all had endured hardships right along the side of their other while she was going through them.

On December 23rd of that year their deepest fear came true, it was time to gather all the grandchildren together to tell them their mom mom was gone to be with the lord. Karly was only six years old at

the time just sat their very still and very quiet as she along with the rest of her cousins and watched their parents, aunts and uncles hold their tears back even though they could see the sorrow in all the adult's eyes. This day marked the day in

Karly's life that changed everything as she seen it. Her cousin Melissa who had a face shaped like Snoopy with a mocha color skin complexion whispered then she didn't want to live with her daddy anymore, but she wanted to go stay with her mother for good.

    Months passed and the house she knew as her grandma's house began to change. It wasn't the same loving comfortable place she once knew it to be. Karly's mother along with her two sisters then moved into a three-bedroom apartment not far from where her grandma once lived. This was a new neighborhood in which Karly had to make new friends and most importantly get used to having her own room because she never had her own room when she lived at her grandma's house all the children shared one big room. So, she knew it was going to take some getting used to, but she also knew it would be just fine living there with her mother and two sisters. The one thing Karly remembered her grandmother telling her was when you're the oldest you must always protect your younger siblings, so this is what Karly had to take on as the oldest of her mother's children.

    Karly was used to Alice because after all her and Alice were only two years apart, but she had to get used to having a little brother named Antoine. Alice was a short dark skin little girl with a whole lot of hair and a fat face. Antoine was a short skinny little boy whose clothes fell off him every day no matter if he had a belt on or not. He could probably stand beside a pole and never be seen is how skinny he was. Antoine was one of those kids that made Karly want to lock in the closet somewhere because he always had something to say regardless of if her was wrong or not. So, growing up living in this apartment was going to be a learning experience for Karly, however not a day went by that she didn't look up to the sky and talk to her grandma especially when she was out in awkward situations.

    To Karly once her mom-mom passed away, she felt as though so much began to happen to her or around her she figured it was something she did wrong. Karly's mother began working a couple of jobs at a time to make sure she could make a living for her and her three children. Chandra which was Karly's mother had a friend who would watch Karly and her siblings for her while she worked both jobs to make money and provide for her babies. Karly was very overprotective of her siblings, so she didn't hesitate to take up for them once so ever. Chandra's girlfriends name was Janet, who had a husband named Tyrone and three children of her own all ranging around the same ages of Chandra's children so that really worked out just fine. Janet was a real skinny chick who didn't weigh more than a wet paper bag. She kind of reminded Karly of Gismo from the movie Gremlins with the shape of her eyes, and nose and how she wore her hair.

    Chandra had been raising her kids to be very well mannered and to obey all adults when they were supposed to. Sometimes Chandra would pull double shifts at one job and must be right back at her other job early in the morning so at times Karly and her siblings spent the night at Janet's house. Once time passed Karly and her siblings had learned

7

the ways around Janet's house, as they noticed her kids did right what they wanted to do and hardly ever got in trouble. Her kids would do

stuff and blame it on Karly and her siblings knowing they weren't raised to do half of the crap those little bad behind kids did. One day Janet's son Leroy had broken a window out of the house next door, and he blamed Karly for it, so Janet made Karly come in the house for a while for punishment. Karly fell asleep while being on punishment and when she woke up Tyrone Janet's husband was touching her. Tyrone was kind of muscular with curly black hair and a long face shaped like a stretched bubble. He told Karly if she told anyone they wouldn't believe her so she didn't say a word, thinking that it wouldn't matter much because all he did was touch her. Not thinking anything of its Karly brushed it off and went on outside to chill with the rest of the crew.

Little did Karly know this was only the beginning, the obstacles that lie ahead for her as she grew up. Karly and her siblings attended frequent visits to Janet's up until she was of age. Tyrone knew Karly wouldn't open her mouth and say anything, and every time she threatens to tell on him, he would tell her if she didn't let him do what he wanted with her then he would just do it with Alice. Karly was very overprotective of her younger siblings and before she allowed Tyrone to touch Alice, she would do whatever Tyrone instructed her to do. It got to the point where she knew what he wanted when he wanted it before he even gave her instructions. She would then go home and stand in the shower for what seemed like forever just to get the feeling of filth off her. All she knew was she'd be damned she let anything happen to Alice. Even though Alice was a pain in Karly's ass from time to time she remembered as the oldest

she was to protect her younger siblings and she did just that. After a while Chandra had gotten a better job in their hometown which meant Karly never had to see Janet or Tyrone ever again in her life which made her very happy, and that uneasy feeling went away finally. To Karly the death of her grandma brought her nothing but bad stuff, one thing after another. This made her feel like she had to keep the most disrespectful demeanor a young girl could ever have. Karly didn't yet understand why such bogus crap was happening to her "I mean what the hell did I do" is what Karly often asked herself day in and day out. Thing is what she didn't know was it was going to take several more years and several more experiences she had to go through before that answer would eventually come to her.

    While years went by Chandra continued to work her ass off to make sure Karly, Alice, and Antoine had everything they needed and some of what they wanted. Karly was older than she was when Chandra first started to really work more than one job a time, so now she didn't need a babysitter. They could all stay right home, and their neighbor would watch the apartment to make sure they didn't come out or let anybody in while Chandra went to work. One evening Chandra came home and told Karly she had gotten word that her father had been released from prison and wanted to come gets her for a night. Chandra was asking Karly what she thought about that and if she really wanted to go. Karly now about twelve years old told her mother she would let her know once she thought about it. The topic was left alone and would be picked up later when Karly was ready to address it and Chandra knew that so being the mother, she was she didn't say anything else about it. Chandra was a beautiful 32-year-old mother of three. She was what the guys called a redbone with a pretty face and a voluptuous figure in the shape of any hourglass with just a tad bit of baby fat left on her. She could pull any kind of man she wanted but she just was a laid-back individual who was strictly about her kids.

 A week or so had gone buy and still no word from Karly about whether she wanted to meet her dad and go spend a night with him. At this point Chandra who really didn't want to bring up the conversation first but had given Karly what she thought was more than enough time to think about this. As they had sat down to eat dinner that evening as everyone took a turn to talk about how their day had gone in school up popped the conversation and to Chandra surprise Karly had started it as she hoped she would. Karly stated that she was tired of hearing all the other kids in school speak about what they get to do with their dads, so she wanted to have something to go back to school Monday morning to brag about as well.

  After dinner that evening Chandra contacted that very person who could pass the message for her to Karly's dad for him to pick her up Friday evening. Oh boy Karly shouted as she heard her mother on the phone speaking with someone who knew her dad, she rushed upstairs to plan her evening with her dad because she knew it would be an awesome one. Karly figured if she had to go through all that crap before her mother found a better job than a fun night was well deserved without having any worry's. That night when Karly laid down for bed, she said her prayers and dreamed about the great time

10

she was going to have with her dad. She thought about all the questions she was going to ask him and all the places they were going to get to go together. She was going to have loads to tell her friends at school on Monday.

    Friday had soon arrived, and Karly got up and ready for school that morning very quickly. She was ready for the day to start and go by so she could hurry up and get back home to pack for the evening with her daddy. After arriving at school Karly went on with her day as usual, doing work, having recess after lunch which always marked the middle of the day and then off to the rest of her classes. Before she knew it seventh period had swung around which meant they were just about done for the day because eighth period she went back to her homeroom class to prepare for dismissal. Once home Karly began to pack for her evening with her dad and she was overly excited because she had only seen pictures of him in letters, she had gotten from him. They had never meant face to face, so it was like a very big present for Karly. After all these years she was finally going to meet the man who helped create her this was by far the best moment of her life, and she was beyond ready for it. All there was left for her to do was wait for her mom to check her clothes and make sure she had everything packed she needed for that one evening. Chandra examined the bag and once she seen everything Karly needed was in there, she told her that he would be there to pick her up at 6pm. All Karly had to do was sit back and wait for him to emerge.

11

It was well after 6pm and Karly's dad hadn't gotten there to pick her up yet, so she began to grow impatient and tired. Her mother had told her to go set and play the Nintendo 64 with her siblings to keep from her having such a sad look on her face. Karly and her siblings played the game for another hour or so when suddenly a hard solid knock came upon the door. The room grew quiet as Chandra went to answer the door. Karly immediately began to feel butterflies in her stomach as her mother unlocked the top lock and then the bottom lock. Suddenly the door opened just a tad bit enough for Karly to see what seemed to be a slightly thin figure on the other side of the door asking if he could come in.

Chapter 2

The door opened and in walked a medium build man with a bold head and a few blemishes on his face entered the house. His skin was like the color of an almond. Chandra called Karly to come over to where they stood and introduced her to her father Jonathan. Jonathan hadn't seen Karly since she was between the ages of two and four, so she didn't remember him. Karly just looked with astonishment because it was as if her dream was finally coming true and she knew she would have something to return to school Monday morning and tell all those who were always talking about things they get to do with their dads. She would finally fit in with the kids who were growing up in the same house with their dads even though she was only going to spend one night with her dad.

A few moments later out the door Karly went with her bag of clothes and a few things she wanted to do with her dad while they were together. Jonathan and Karly really didn't say much as they walked to his vehicle. Upon arriving at the car Karly noticed a woman and two children inside. Jonathan took Karly's belongings and placed them in the trunk as she got in the back beside the kids. One of them smelled funny as Karly noticed and the other one just sat there staring at her. Karly began to feel very sad because she didn't know anybody in that car not even the man who was introduced to her as her father.

13

    Finally, the car began to back out and Karly seen her mom go back inside of their house and her eyes got watery, however she didn't cry just sighed to herself. She missed her mom already, but she knew she would be home the next evening. Karly thought she might as well learn some things about her dad because she knew nothing about him but his name, even though his mother always made sure she informed Karly about him. Jonathan's mother was always coming to get Karly and taking her to her store to buy all sorts of things, just so that Karly would know his side of her family was around the same area she was growing up in. As the car was riding everybody was silent listening to the music from the cassette player.

    After 30 to 45 minutes, they had finally arrived at the place Karly's dad called home. The car was placed in park, and everyone began to exit the vehicle one by one. Karly looked around to see she was at some type of apartment complex. There were about eight dudes standing out by a pole shooting dice. Jonathan asked the one guy they called Don if he was ready to have his money taken? Don replied "N-I-G-G-A please", and Jonathan just laughed. Once everyone was in the house Jonathan and his girlfriend Erica asked Karly what she would like to eat? Karly replied chicken and fries with some grape Kool aid if you have it, please. Erica's son James and daughter Emily shouted yayyyy!!! So,

Erica didn't have to ask them what they wanted for dinner.

14

Once Karly, Emily and James had eaten it was time for them all to take their baths so they could get ready for bed. Karly spent her bath time thinking of things to talk about with her dad but really couldn't come up with anything. She figured she'd just wing it once she got the chance to do so. Jonathan really wasn't sure what to say to his daughter either, so he started off by asking her what she liked to do? Karly was so excited because right then she had the chance to inform her father of how great she was at playing any sport. They laughed and joked around for about an hour or so and then he tucked her in kissed her on her forehead and told her goodnight. Karly was still so very much excited it was hard for her to settle down and go to sleep, so she replayed that little bit of time spent talking with her dad over and over in her head as she finally drifted off to sleep.

    Screech.... Hours later Karly heard the door open to where she was sleeping, and she rolled over to see who it was. She figured it was either Erica or Jonathan peeping in to see if she was asleep, so she just closed her eyes back and pretended as if she were still asleep figuring that whomever it was would see she was asleep and close the door to go back to bed. The door was eventually closed, and Karly started drifting back to sleep when she felt a hand moving up her leg to her private area, from there up to her newly forming breasts. Karly turned to see that it was Jonathan and she begged him to stop. Karly said, "my dad why is you doing this to me"? Jonathan's replied you're a big girl so it will be ok. Karly tried to get away thinking to herself this shit can't possibly be happening to me again. She could smell the alcohol and cigarette smell from Jonathan all the way across the other side of the room. He had locked the door and there was no window, she had

no way of escaping this situation. Tears streaming down Karly's face as she tried to talk the man who she was supposed to call dad from raping her. Jonathan told Karly the only way she was going to be able to go back to sleep was if she gave him what he was there to get. He then explained to her that this moment was the only reason he came to get her. Karly's tears rolled even more down her face as Jonathan began to approach her as he pinned her on the wall licking her tears from her face. Karly trembled with fear as Jonathan removed her shorts and panties while holding her against the wall by her throat. He picked her up and placed his hands under her as he entered her, she cried and fought him to let her go. He then threw her down on the bed and had his way with her for about two hours and she cried and cried "please let me go". It seemed like this nightmare lasted forever to Karly as she cried so many tears stopped falling because she went from literally crying to crying on the inside.

Once Jonathan had finished, he told Karly who was laying on her stomach that if she ever spoke of this night to anyone, he would find her and kill her, Chandra, Alice and Antione. When morning came Karly was very sore, but she had to keep it together, because all she could hear was him threatening to kill her and her family if she spoke of the nightmare she lived in the wee hours of that morning.

Karly made sure she didn't show any signs that something happened to her just hours ago while everyone else was sleeping peacefully. She attempted to walk normal and act as if nothing was wrong. She'd been down this very same road years prior so she knew how to not show any type of clue that could lead up to exposing Jonathan for what he really was. As time went by, she found herself asking Erica when were they planning to take her home? Erica then asked Jonathan what time they were going to be leaving, his response was "whenever my baby girl is ready to leave, we can go." Karly sat there amazed because this man had no remorse in his eyes or voice. He didn't even try to apologize to her for what he had done. Karly spoke out and said "I'm ready to go home now" with a bit of anger in her voice and hatred in her eyes.

    Jonathan grabbed the keys and told everybody to get their coats on, while he went to warm up the car. At that very moment Erica asked Karly if she alright.

Karly nodded and spoke softly "yes". She then took her bag and through the soda can in the trash and slowly walked out the door looking forward to returning home to Chandra. As they rode down the highway Karly quickly set a plan into motion. She knew her mother was going to ask how everything went with her and Jonathan. So, Karly figured she'd tell her mother they played video games, ate pizza, watched movies and went to bed and in that order.

    Shortly after arriving back home, Karly hugged her mother and proceeded to put her dirty clothes away so she could get ready for school in the morning. Chandra decided to wait once again and allow Karly to tell her all about the time she spent with Jonathan, Erica, and her kids. Surprisingly Karly never said a word about it, which was a bit strange to Chandra because Karly left her the day before overly excited about spending the night with Jonathan for the first time. While sitting at the table Alice asked "Karly what did y'all do at

your dad's house"? The thought of what happened to Karly almost made her gag while eating dinner, but she held it in. Karly finished chewing her food and said, "oh well we played video games, ate pizza, watched movies, and went to bed" just as she had rehearsed in her mind. Chandra then followed up saying "that seemed like you had fun". Yeah, it was alright I guess said Karly. Deep down inside she is crying like a baby because she was violated for the second time in her entire 18 years of being on the face of the earth.

Karly didn't let that stop her from excelling in every sport she played while in middle school. She took it as a lesson well learned, although her attitude started to spiral out of control. She found herself in all sorts of fights, class disruptions, and suspensions from school. Although Karly was an excellent athlete her temper was terrible, so the guidance counselors and some teachers started to work with her on how to channel her anger in other ways instead of starting a fight every time she disagreed with another student. As time went on and Karly got older, she found herself always keeping busy, because when she wasn't busy those horrible thoughts tend to seep in, and she would begin to cry. Not very many people had ever seen Karly cry, because she always made sure that she didn't let anybody get to close to her.

The way she saw it was, why should she give anybody the time of the day to get to know her when all they were going to do was hurt her in the end. When Karly entered her senior year, no matter how she felt boys started to look more then like toys to her. As it happens with every 18-year-old teenage girl. Karly never really thought about boys before that night. The only time guys crossed her mind was when she'd stare off in a daze wondering how it would have been to have grown up

with a real dad who was the total opposite of hers. It really didn't matter anymore to Karly now because she was a teenager who knew she didn't have time for no bullshit from those of the opposite sex. She had been hurt too many times so the way she looked at it was she going to get hers before they get there's.

   A little way into her senior year she started to receive little notes from a guy on the varsity basketball team. The notes were cute and all, but Karly didn't have time for any games. She had noticed him flirting with a lot of other girls, so it didn't make her feel special getting notes from him. Though he was a dark skin brother with a slim build he put Karly in mind of the actor Morris Chestnut who was so sexy to her she couldn't help but indulge in his little letter game to see how far it would go. Little did she know from the first letter she wrote back only piqued his interest even the more about her. He noticed she wasn't like the rest of the girls, who were willing to do whatever just to say they have been with one of the school jocks. Karly was in no rush to feel what she remembered to be the most painful feeling she'd ever felt.

As she sat in the library reading a book, she heard this deep but sexy voice whisper in her ear "how busy are you really little mama"? Karly turned around and there stood Jamal with his tall, slightly built self-smiling down at her. She looked up into his eyes and thought to herself damn he is so fine as she smiled and said, "not real busy more like bored trying to pass time". It was the end of the day and Karly was ready to go home and rest since there was no field hockey practice that day because it was a Friday. Jamal asked her if he could

take her home after school, and as good as it sounded Karly said no thank you. In which she believed would make him walk away and leave her alone. She had heard all about Jamal and the guys he hung around with, but something about him was very intriguing which made Karly tell him she might take him up on that offer the next time. Jamal's face went from a frown to a smile, and he said, "ok I'll keep that in mind little mama, hope we can talk again sometime soon". Jamal said as he gently walked away. Karly's heart skipped what seemed like a thousand beats and at that very moment the last bell rang which meant the weekend had finally arrived. She grabbed her books and went on to her bus. On the ride home she thought about Jamal and suddenly remembered he had written his number down in a couple of those letters he passed her.

After getting home and settled, Karly lay across her bed and started to replay the end of her day while smiling a very big Kool aid smile. She wondered if she should be the first to call him or if she ought to let him make the first move. Ring Ring Ring....... Ring Ring Ring.... the house phone is starts to ring and it's her home girl Chanel. She's asking Karly what was up with Jamal and her sitting talking in the library before the bell rang. "Damn Chanel you noisy as hell girl" replied Karly. But since you asked it wasn't much of anything he asked a question and I answered it Karly added. Umm Hmm Chanel responds back you know they say he got a nice one girl....... Oh well Karly says I am not looking for any boyfriend, screw buddy, phone sex buddy, none of that. As I stated he asked a question and I answered it, with a bit of anger in her voice. Chanel said, "damn girl calms down, any way is your mom home yet"? Na not yet why what's cracking for

20

today asked Karly. Not much of shit girl just chilling for now call me when your mom get home so we can get up and chill a bit before dark Chanel replied. I got you Karly said later Nell....... Karly hung up the house phone and started to think even more about calling Jamal especially after what Chanel was talking about. Nope I'm not calling him Karly said in her mind no no no no..........

    As Chandra comes through the door, Karly waits for her to get settled and asked her mom if she would drop her off at Chanel house for a little while. Even though Karly and Chanel never did much of anything but walk around and see what they could see, with a little bit of an occasional flirt with the guys when they saw them. Chandra told Karly once she took her shower and all she would gladly drop her off at Chanel's house as long as Chanel's mother Ms. Tyra didn't mind. Ms. Tyra was older than Chandra but they both came up with the same type of upbringing after all they grew up in the same town. Ms. Tyra was around the same ages of Karly's Aunt Lorraine and Aunt Betsy who were way older than Chandra. After about an hour or so Chandra was ready to take Karly around Chanel's while she goes to run errands. Alice and Antione will stay with Chandra because after all Karly is now a senior in high school, so she had a bit more freedom and was trusted to do the right thing as she was brought up to do.

Once Karly had gotten dropped off at Chanel's house, they started their little walk around the town of Gaithersburg. They normally just walked, talked, flirted occasionally with the boys around their town and relaxed. On this day Jamal and his crew were at the carwash chilling watching to see who all walked through there. When Jamal spotted Karly, he started to smile that sexy ass smile he gave her

in the library. To keep from blushing Karly kept talking to Chanel, who was saying girl his boys are dogs but cute ones though......... As they both busted out laughing loud enough for them to all stop and turn around to find out what was so funny. Jamal asked what was so damn funny? Chanel was like nothing's funny Karly was just saying something to me that I found funny so we both laughed and why is it any of y'all business? Chanel snapped back. Chanel had a very outspoken personality and she used it faithfully by any means which is why her and Karly seen eye to eye. Both young ladies had already been through a lot in life, so they didn't play games with anyone.

    Jamal walked over to the girls and asked Chanel if she would excuse him and Karly for a moment as they stepped to the side to chat a little. Chanel said Karly if you need me, I'll be over here talking to my cousin Mike. As Karly walked over to the side with Jamal where nobody could see them, he stood her up against the wall and asked her why she was playing so hard to get with him? Karly thought to herself she doesn't trust no male or the shit they say but looking into his eyes she somehow knew he was different. She answered saying she didn't know and that it was a habit. Once again, they stood over there talking laughing and he told her he would like to take her somewhere with him the next day. Karly told him she would have to ask her mom, he said how about I ask her myself. This shocked Karly because Jamal was willing to come to her house and ask Chandra if he could take her somewhere. She didn't believe he would, so she said whatever and walked back over to Chanel as they began to continue their daily walk.

Chapter 3

Night was approaching, Channel and Karly knew it was about time to get to either one of the houses they were the closest too. Whether it was Chanel's house or Karly house they both basically had the same curfew, to be in the house before it became dark out. What Karly didn't know was Chandra had sent someone to pick her up from Chanel's house and take her home because she was running a bit behind schedule. She had called Chanel's mom and told her Karly's cousin Ciara was picking her up to take her home. When Ciara got there Karly told Chanel she would call her later and got into Ciara's car and left. Karly was telling her big cousin all about Jamal along with some of the things he had said to her. Ciara asked how he acted towards her around his boys and Karly told her the same way he does when the two of them are alone. Ciara's response was taken it slow and don't do anything she wasn't ready for. Most importantly Ciara told Karly the word NO was a powerful word, and all guys should except that word when it's spoken to them. Not long after they arrived back at Karly's house. Ciara let her out, watched to make sure she made it in the house with no problem and backed out to go on about her business.

   Months passed Jamal became a regular face around Karly's neighborhood. The two of them would go out to eat, movies and just ride around enjoying laughs and talking about life after high school. Chandra like Jamal so much that he could even come over her house when she wasn't at home. Jamal's mother was friends with one of Karly's uncles and his sons played on the little league team with Jamal

23

and his brother Raheem. One evening Jamal and Karly were kissing in the car and it started getting hot between the two, Jamal asked Karly if she was sure she was ready? Karly hadn't ever been touched so gently before and she enjoyed it, so she said yes, she was ready. They went back to Jamal's house where they would be all alone, and he laid her down on his bed kissing her softly all over her body. He carefully removed her clothing piece by piece until she was completely naked. He then removed his clothes, and when Karly got a glance of his manhood her mouth dropped as she thought to herself "where the hell is he going to put that?"

Jamal started to rub and caress Karly causing her to squirm all over the bed as he reached for a condom. He then put it on and while kissing her ears, neck, and lips he gently inserted himself inside of her. Karly let out a real loud moan and Jamal gentle worked himself from side to side with a stroke that drove Karly crazy. This was her first time she ever willingly gave herself away and it felt damn good. She moaned and groaned as he moved faster and faster bringing himself to an orgasm within 30 minutes. After he was done, he took off the condom and started to kiss her passionately all over as he reached for another condom this time, he laid on his back and showed Karly how to reach her peak of climax.

About an hour and a half had gone by and Jamal and Karly had fell asleep. The house phone rang, when Jamal answered with a groggy voice it was his mom saying she wouldn't be home until morning and for him and his brother to eat leftovers and clean the kitchen afterwards. Karly had awakened a bit sore from all the sex they had, and she was feeling exhausted but in a great way.

24

   Karly and Jamal then started to officially date and everybody knew of it. Chanel asked Karly if she had given him any, and Karly just smiled. Usually they speak about everything, so Chanel couldn't understand why Karly hadn't told her she had given it up to Jamal. Karly on the other hand understood exactly why she hadn't told Chanel. She learned a long time ago that everything isn't for everybody, so telling her best friend she finally gave up the goodies was too much information for her to know. Jamal and Karly became even closer as time went on even though Karly knew he flirted with other girls and all she didn't care if it wasn't done in her face. That would cause a very big problem.

    The Christmas dance was approaching, and Karly waited for Jamal to ask her if she wanted to attend the dance with him. She knew she wanted to go with him but wasn't sure he felt the same way due to the fact she caught him having sex with another female. Karly had fell in love with Jamal, besides that she knew he had fell in love with her too, however he was still young and dumb as high school boys tend to be. Eventually Jamal was tired of getting the cold shoulder from Karly, so he went to her house one evening to sweet talk her, so he thought.

A knock came on the door, Karly told Alice to see who was at the door and so she did. While sitting in the living room watching one of her favorite movies, she noticed Alice and Antoine were playing and laughing. As Karly looked up her entire demeanor changed, Jamal had gotten her attention just as he planned. "WHAT ARE YOU DOING HERE?" Karly snapped. Jamal responding, "saying I came to talk to you will you step outside with me?" Chandra then stepped in and said go ahead Karly and see what the young man would like to talk about.

Karly knew her mother was very fond of Jamal, however she never told Chandra how much of a male whore he was. Karly loved Jamal and he knew that so whenever he got caught up doing shit, he always attempted to sweet talk Karly into forgiving him. Telling her how much he loved her and how dumb he was for messing up something so good. It took time but eventually Karly would forgive Jamal and fall in love with him all over deeper than before.

    It's now been about two and a half months since Karly had caught Jamal and it was right back to his old tricks. He had waited for her afterschool one day and when she got in the car, she noticed Jamal had changed his clothes. He had basketball practice later that evening, so she sat quietly wondering why he had changed clothes so early. Karly never said anything she just sat on the passenger side staring out the window. When they arrived at Jamal house his brother met us at the door saying, "Mal man you ready to be caught up". Jamal says man whatever by passing his brother with Karly right behind him as they walked down the hall. He instructs Karly to go in him bedroom while he goes to see what the hell his brother is talking about. In the mist of all that Karly heard another female's voice in the living room so she came out the room. It was a girl named Monica who Karly had already exchanged words with over Jamal.

    Immediately Karly asked Jamal "what the hell is she doing here"? Jamal was once again at lost for words. So, Karly turned around went back in the room grabbing all her shit and walked out the back door. Jamal left Monica standing in the middle of the living room to run behind her. He went to spend Karly around telling her it wasn't anything like she was thinking. "WELL, WHAT THE HELL IS IT THEN

26

JAMAL?" Karly shouted. "I'M SICK OF THIS SHIT AND IF YOU WANT THAT BITCH, YOU CAN HAVE HER!!!" Karly stated as she walked down the lane leaving Jamal's house. At that moment Jamal knew Karly was done and not to try the basic getting back together routine he normally tries when he screws up badly. Jamal and Karly really were an item as the older folks said but Karly was tired of loving someone who would possibly never love her back in the same way. As she cried walking down the street, she called Chanel and told her to come pick her up letting her know exactly where she was. When Chanel finally arrived Karly had damn near walk almost to her house which was a few miles from Jamal's. Chanel asked Karly what happened noticing she had been crying, her response was short and sweet "I'm single and I'm good." Chanel knew Karly and knew how she felt about Jamal, also knew when Karly was ready to talk about it, she would be the one she talked about it to. Karly sat quietly in the car as Chanel talked and talked even though they were a few miles from Karly house the trip felt like it had been hours. With all sorts of things rushing through Karly's head, it took all she had to hold her tears back while sitting in the car with Chanel.

 Finally approaching her house Karly sits out in the car and stared into space with so many questions about life and why negative things always happen to her. After taking a long deep breath she tells Chanel she'll call her sometime in the morning once she gets herself together. Chanel responds "bet luv". Karly exits the car fiddling in her bag for her house keys when she notices a set of headlights coming down the road. She knew Chanel had already pulled out the yard so immediately Karly started saying "I hope this car isn't for me" "I hope

27

this car isn't for me" over and over in her head, even though deep down she already knew it was. Finally finding her keys in her bag she hurry's and opens the door shut it and went to her room after telling Chandra she was home. Chandra looked at the time and wondered what in the world was going on because Karly was never in the house this early on a Friday night.

"Whewww that was close" Karly said as she through her belongings on her bed. She looked at her clock on her stand and realized it was super early, her curfew wasn't until ten o'clock, so she decided to take a shower and attempted to relax her mind. Karly stood in the shower as the water ran thinking about whether she should go out after getting herself together or sit in the house with her family. Once finished showering Karly headed back to her room while passing the stairs, she heard her mother talking to somebody, so she figured Chandra was on the house phone. While listening to her slow jams Karly was looking for something cute to put on for the evening. It was just about early winter, and she knew wherever she went she would most likely be outside. Keeping all that in mind Karly picked out a cute, hooded fleece that was navy blue and white with a pair of nicely fitting jeans and her timberlands. She reapplied her makeup and pulled her braids up in a ponytail slicking down her edges. Karly's caramel complexion was as beautiful as ever, but she still was heartbroken. As she listened to all the slow jams on her cd, she couldn't help but to think about all the things she had been through while dealing with Jamal. Karly turned off the slow jams at that moment and said to herself bump that. It's my turn to enjoy myself and go on a few dates with someone other than Jamal for once.

Finally, Karly emerges from her room and heads downstairs to let her mother know she will be stepping back out for a little while. As she approached the final step, she recognizes the voice clearly and it's her mom's friend from work Gloria. Karly speaks to Gloria as she says, "just the young lady I came to see'. Karly stands there stuck wondering "what the hell does this fool want with me?" Chandra then tells Karly that Gloria's nephew is down for a while and doesn't know anybody their age, and she would like her to show him around. Karly had enough on her mind and really didn't want to be caught around some geek with her bad girl image. Before Karly muttered anything out her mouth Chandra told her at least meet him before being mean saying no. That's the least Karly could do for her mom, so Gloria went out to the car, while Karly walked into the kitchen to see what Chandra had in there for dinner. She wondered what this nigga could really look like because Gloria wasn't what one would call attractive at all. She was very dark and heavy built with a nose like Miss Piggy and sounded like the lady from married with children. Her face looked like a pizza with a bunch of pimples so she could only imagine what Gloria's nephew looked like.

 The door opens and shuts quickly, and Karly hears this deep voice saying, "nice to meet you Ms. Chandra". "Damn!! Karly says that nigga sounds good as hell". She knows she best not let Chandra hear her curse. Karly Chandra says come here and meet Gloria's nephew Rashad, okay here I come Karly replies. When Karly turned the corner leaving out of the kitchen her mouth dropped, knees got weak, and words were lost all at once. Gloria says "Rashad this is Karly, Karly this is Rashad". Rashad says "hello Karly nice to finally meet you" with his hand extended out to shake her hand. Karly still lost for words says in a shy like manner "hi". Chandra asked her daughter was she okay to go out because she looked a little fragile just then. Karly assured her mother she was just fine, asking Rashad if he would like to walk out around town with her. He nodded and out the door they went. Karly starting out her yard thinking to herself damn how could someone so beautiful be related to Miss piggy talking about Gloria. Rashad was 18 years old about 6ft tall muscular frame, a caramel skin tone and looked almost just like Shamar Moore from the stories, but with a bit more thug in him. As the two teenagers walked Rashad started to open about himself and why he was sent to live with his aunt. Karly just listened and observed the way he moved and how he carried himself. He was indeed a gentleman because he walked on the outside while Karly walked closer to the grass. Karly out the blue asked Rashad if she could ask him a question from a male perspective. Rashad nodded yes. Karly begins to talk about the relationship she has been in for the past several months that was just ended earlier that day. She said to Rashad "why do you guys cheat on good girls for those whoring chicks who have slept with dozens of different guys?" Rashad started laughing which made Karly angry, so she stopped and looked at him asking "what's so funny?" Rashad wasn't laughing at her situation just at the fact that he is a teenage guy who has done the very same thing to a female. He told Karly he didn't have an answer for her question, which left he is pondering even the more as they approached the stores in town.

30

The first-person Rashad and Karly ran into was her best friend, Chanel. Chanel was in the store when Rashad walked in and turned the heads of every female in the store. Chanel said, "Karly girl did you see that fine ass nigga that just walked in the store?" Karly playing a long said "no where he at Chanel?" When he walked out the store and started walking in their direction Karly said, "who that nigga right there?" Chanel said, "damn right that nigga right there". "Oh, shit girl that's just Rashad" replied Karly. At that moment it was only a matter of time before Chanel started with the fifty questions. Before Chanel even got the chance Rashad introduced himself as a friend of Karly's also mentioning he was Gloria's nephew.

 As the three of them started to sit at the carwash and talk a bit passing time Jamal rode by, damn near hitting the car in front of him while starring at Rashad as he sat talking to Karly and Chanel. Instead of him going straight through the light Jamal decided to turn and pull up in the carwash to wash his car. "Yo Chanel" called Jamal Chanel looks and says, "I wonder what the hell this nigga wants". Karly, I bet he asks me who Rashad mumbled Chanel is. "Yeah, I bet" Karly said with anger as she and Rashad sat chatting about their lives trading stories and sharing laughs while passing time. After walking all around town Karly decided she was getting a bit tired of the regular and was seriously considering taking it in for the rest of the evening when Rashad asked her if she would like to take a ride with him. "Now how do you insist we do that with no car" Karly snapped. Rashad answers "chill baby girl I have a car and license". The thought of having time all alone with Rashad was very exciting Karly thought because she

was really attracted to him but didn't want to come off as being fast like those very same girls they discussed earlier in the evening. As they reached Gloria's house Karly noticed a ford expedition with rims sitting in the driveway. Rashad unlocked the doors and started the truck up to warm up while he went inside the house. Jamal's car had nothing on this SUV and Karly loved it. She knew he had already questioned Chanel in which he really didn't find out much because she didn't know much Karly smiled at the thought of Jamal wondering about what's going on between her and Rashad.

There wasn't anything going on but keeping him guessing was a lot of fun for Karly considering he had cheated so many times and made her cry just as many times if not more. She decided she was going to milk this situation if she could just to make Jamal look like a jackasss. After dwelling in her thought the driver side door opened and Rashad hopped up in the truck. "Baby girl are you ready to take a ride?" asked Rashad. Karly shook her head and off they went. While the loud music thumped through the speakers Karly just sat looking around as Rashad drove through town. They noticed Chanel was still at the carwash with a stunning look upon her face as they pulled up to ask her if she wanted a ride home. Jamal's face was tight as Rashad spoke "what's up man I'm Rashad". Jamal looked over at Karly and back at Rashad saying, "nigga I don't give a damn who you are, all I want to know is why my girl in your truck?" Karly turned her head in Chanel's direction asking her was she ready to go or what totally ignoring Jamal which pissed him off even more. Chanel told Karly her friend was just about there because they were going on a date to the movies. That sounds like a great idea Rashad announced, Karly would

32

you like to go to the movies this evening Rashad asked with a devilish grin on his face looking directly at Jamal. Karly said, "I'm down for whatever Rashad it's boring just riding around town". Rashad looked over at Karly and smiled with the thought damn we finally can be alone now I can get to know her better. As they rode off Karly seen Chanel get in the car with her friend and watched as Jamal got in his car pulling away from the carwash. Karly didn't have enough money for the movies she told Rashad and his response was amazingly perfect. He told Karly whatever she wanted she could have all he wanted to do was enjoy her company whenever she was available for him to do so. This comment shocked Karly being she had only just met Rashad hours earlier.

   They swung by Karly's house to let Chandra know they were going to leave out of town and would return later after the movie. Chandra replied be safe and mind your manners you too. Finally, a night out without a bunch of crap from Jamal, Karly was overly excited. Rashad was a Shai fanatic, so they listened to them the entire time they rode that evening. Shockingly Karly knew all the words to every song on the cd. The vibe they had was like no other and Karly was sure she wanted to get to know more about Rashad, however at the same time she wondered if he was digging her the same way. Once arriving at the movies, the line for

"Independence Day" was backed up to the road.

    Karly wasn't about to stand in that long line waiting hours to see the movie so she asked Rashad if they could find something else to do. Rashad was all for that, so they got back in the truck considering going to view the movie another time together. Being around Rashad gave

33

    Karly hardly any time to think about Jamal and all the games he had been playing with her heart. As the two walked back to the car Jamal and four of his homies approached them. Rashad made sure he moved Karly to his other side by taking her hand and escorting her in plain sight. "Damn Mal that nigga just straight whored you man what you going to do about that?" shouted David, Jamal's right-hand man. "Na Dave, I'm not going to just let that happen." Jamal mumbled as Karly and Rashad were walking past him. Jamal swung and Rashad fell to the grown. The rest of them began to kick and punch Rashad over and over until he laid unconscious on the sidewalk.

    Karly dropped to her knees crying begging them to stop beating Rashad. She told Jamal she wouldn't see Rashad anymore if he just left him alone. Sirens getting closer, Jamal and the rest of the boys took off running in the opposite direction. Karly sat there awaiting the arrival of the ambulance as she cried on the phone telling Gloria what has happened. Gloria was still at Karly's house with Chandra sitting back talking after a long week of work. Chandra and Gloria told Karly to go ahead and go to the hospital with Rashad and they would meet her them there.

Chapter 4

    She sat in the waiting room for what seemed to be hours and hours while replaying her evening over and over in her mind. Each time more tears rolled out of her eyes. For once she thought God had sent her somebody, she finally felt appreciated her and this is what happens. Karly wondered what she did so wrong in her life to be dealt such a bullshit hand. She knew she couldn't handle anymore situations that made her feel like it was all her fault. She began to think about Rashad and how he wouldn't be in this situation if she had only stayed to talk with Jamal, the night wouldn't have ended on these terms. "Paging Doctor Johnson, paging Doctor Johnson" spoken loudly over the intercom, snapping Karly out of her daze.

    Looking up she spotted Chandra and Gloria talking to the nurses at the desk. Karly sat there stiff as a board. There was nothing nobody could say to her that would make her feel this wasn't her fault.

Gloria walked over to Karly and hugged her whispering in her ear everything is going to be just fine child. Karly said OK out loud but was thinking in her mind how she was going to find a way to get Jamal back for his ignorance. Karly called Chanel and started to tell her what had happened to Rashad. Chanel couldn't believe it; she didn't think Jamal had a thuggish seed in his body because he was more of a lover. "Yo come pick me up from the hospital Nel we got something to get done mama" Karly said quietly so Chandra and Gloria couldn't hear her. "Not a problem chica I'm on my way" Chanel responded. "Hey mom I'm about to go with Chanel and attempt to elevate my mind if that's ok" softly Karly spoke. "Oh, okay baby is you going to be alright?" Chandra replied. Yes, ma'am Karly responded walking out the double doors of the hospital. She walked a little way from the hospital so she could spark up a cigarette out of the pack Rashad had brought while they were on their way to the movies. Karly was ready to flip the fuck out and she knew it. Her temper was one thing she couldn't control once she had been pushed so far over the edge. Reaching into her pocket she pulled out her cell phone, strolling down her contacts she gets to Jamal's name and pushes the send button.

    Suddenly Chanel pulls up ranting and raving about Jamal being in a serious car accident and having to be flown out. Karly's heart felt as though it stopped for about three minutes and tears went streaming down her face pouring out of her eyes. Chanel tried to hold her up while her knees became weak, and she fell to the ground. All those negative, nasty thoughts she had about what she was going to say and maybe even do to Jamal were nowhere to be found in Karly's head at this moment. All she could think about was how many times she told him she loved him, and all those times he claimed to love her but hurt her in return. Karly didn't know what else could possibly happen to her in her life at this point. Chanel decided the best thing to do was to take Karly home so she could get herself together. Karly, you have to pull yourself together mama. When Jamal comes out of surgery, he is going to need to see you strong not weak luv he's going to need you Chanel spoke while driving down the highway. Nel when did all of this happen?

"They just beat Rashad up a few hours ago, and now this....". Karly replied. "Why the hell do I have to have the worse shit happen to me Nel huh why me?" cried Karly. It's going to be just fine

36

Karly I'm sure there is an explanation for it all luv I just don't know what it is at this moment, Chanel stated calmly. Karly exits the car in deep thought while walking to her door, tears building up in her eyes while she's fighting to keep them from falling walking through her door. She has never felt so much like she wanted to give up on life as she knew it before this moment, as she lay across her bed mind racing. Her catching Jamal cheating, meeting and getting to know Rashad,

Jamal and his friends jumping Rashad until he was unconscious, and after all of that Jamal being in a very bad car accident happening in one damn day. Only in my life would shit take such drastic measures Karly said wiping her tears as they build up in the corner of her eyes. Karly figured she'd take a hot bath and just clear her mind of everything that has happened thus far and sit by the phone awaiting news about Jamal and Rashad.

    After her hot bath and taking time out to clear her mind the house phone rang, and Karly hurried to answer it. "Hello Karly", Chandra spoke calmly "yes mom I'm here" Karly responded anxiously. Rashad is going to be just fine, a little banged up but fine. Doctors say he has two broken ribs and his lung had just about collapsed but he will pull through just fine. They're going to keep him for a few days to make sure everything is going well before they release him. Chandra sounded really relaxed on the other end of the phone which made Karly be more at ease with his situation. "Mom you know Jamal and his friends put Rashad there all because I caught him with another chick earlier today after school". After you and Gloria introduced Rashad and me, we saw Jamal up at the carwash. Karly figured she'd give her mom a

quick synopsis of how everything went down the best she could. Chandra was shocked listening to Karly explain to her that Rashad was a victim of jealousy. She never thought Jamal was the thuggish type but again there was a lot she didn't know about Jamal. Chandra got so angry listening the gossip Karly was spitting in her ear. Once Karly was done Chandra told her she would finish talking with her once she got home Karly responded ok see you soon and hung up the phone.

    Karly sat patiently on the couch waiting for the house phone, cell phone to ring or even a knock at the door leading to answers about how Jamal was doing now that she knows what's going on with Rashad.......

    WHAM!!!!!...... Karly hopped straight up from her sleep to see what was going on. My fault something was wedged in the door Jamal muttered as he limped on in the living room to Karly. Alice and Antoine came running from their rooms over to

Jamal ready to jump all over him as they do normally when he is there visiting Karly, however they noticed he didn't seem like his normal self. Instead of jumping on him they both asked him if he was okay and once, he answered they went on back to their rooms to continue playing as usual. Jamal sat down across from Karly as she looked at him with a sign of relief seeing he was going to be just fine. Ahhhh Karly let out her sigh as she dropped her head, "what are you doing here Jamal?" she asked. He looked at her with those beautiful eyes she always falls for and stated he had to come see her to find out how Rashad was doing. He then explained to her that the plan was to scare Rashad away from her not to actually physically harm him. Karly felt her anger rising the more Jamal spoke until she finally just screamed "JAMAL GET THE FUCK OUT", you're out here screwing any and every female you possibly can, and you get mad because I have a friend. "JUST GET THE HELL OUT AND LEAVE ME THE HELL ALONE"!!!!! Karly shouted at Jamal as loud as she can causing Chandra to come out of her bedroom to find out what all the screaming going on in her house was about. "Karly Jamal what the hell is going on here?" Chandra spoke as calmly as she could in hopes of getting to the bottom of all this fussing. Nothing mom Jamal was just about to leave and never come back Karly spoke as she tried to calm herself down. Jamal looked Karly in her eyes as he stood up and seen the pain she was feeling as he moved slowly towards the door. Karly left him standing there and went upstairs to her room and began to cry uncontrollably.

    Chandra was left standing their feeling as though she had missed something as she started walking Jamal out. Once Chandra and Jamal reached the door, she told Jamal she had never seen Karly show so much emotion even though it was in a bit of a tantrum before towards anybody. Jamal understood what she was saying and even spoke up and told Chandra he messed up and that this wasn't the first time he hurt Karly. He then asked her mom if she thought Karly meant what she said about him not ever being able to come back? Chandra smiled and said to Jamal give her time to heal and why she is healing you go on exploring and if it's meant for them to cross paths again, they will in time. Chandra hugged Jamal and told him to take care of himself out there in the world, and not to be a stranger. She turned and walked back in the house locking the door behind her.

39

    Chandra didn't even want to bother Karly with all that she had been through, so she just left her alone to gather her thoughts as she had to do many years before her when she and her first true love split. Karly wouldn't ever believe her mother had been heartbroken before either way Chandra looked at it, so she just smiled as she glanced at Karly's bedroom door reminiscing on the good ole days. She knew her daughter would be just fine after all broken hearts were all a part of growing up.

The next morning came and went Karly barely left her room, she felt as though nothing, or no one could enter her world as long as she stayed in her room. "Karly" Chandra shouted from the bottom of the stairs "Alice Antoine and I are going to the flea market would you like to join us"? "Umm.... No, no thank you mom I'll just stay home today if that's alright with you guys". Karly responded in such a gloomy voice. "Well ok then see you when we get back, and if you think of anything you need call my cell", Chandra shouted as they walked out the house. Finally, peace and quiet Karly heads over to her stereo and turns it on, playing was the song "Real Love" by Mary J. Blidge. This gave her a little bit of energy, so she started to pull herself together and make a day out of what was left of the day.

As time went on, she managed to clean up the tissues and things all over her bedroom floor. Opening her windows letting the sunshine through Karly knew she had to move forward and leave all the bad behind her. Well, I guess I'll hop in the shower she thought to herself and then maybe go downstairs and find something on the television to watch. After all it was a weekend and she had nothing better to do.

Chapter 5

Laying across the couch watching Chuck Norris blow everything up in Delta Force a soft knock comes on the door. Karly was a bit puzzled because she heard no vehicle pull up, nor any door close. UGH!!! "Only in my world" Karly sighs as she walks toward the door. "Who is it?" Karly spoke rudely. Karly it's me we need to talk Jamal spoke quietly from the other side of the door. "Go away Jamal" Karly shouted we are done and nothing you can say to me will change that. "Baby I understand that but please let me inside Ms. Chandra said I could come over and check on you so here I am" Jamal spoke with such confidence. "Damn it mom what the hell" .... Karly mumbled as she unlocked the door letting Jamal in the house. SLAM!!!! the door went damn near catching him inside of it. Damn girl, chill out I'm just here to check on you like I told your mom I would do, Jamal stated calmly.

    By the time he starts to get comfortable Karly has tuned him right out as she laid back across the couch and continued to watch her movie. Jamal sat across from her staring trying to find a way to get close to her while they were the only two there. Karly got up to go use the bathroom, which was upstairs, leaving Jamal down in the living room watching tv. Ok Karly gets it together, she mumbled to herself while standing in the mirror. Throwing water on her face Karly stood for a moment then finishing up and heading back to the living room. As she walked down the hall heading to the stairs, she noticed Jamal was up in her room reading her diary. "Jamal why the hell are you up in my room reading my private thoughts like they revolve around you" Karly stated rudely. "Well, I see you hate me and everything I stand for is that true" Jamal asked? "It's there ain't it" Karly smirked.

"Yeah, well I don't believe that why don't you prove you hate me Karly" Jamal smiled. Karly turned to walk away when he grabbed her and started to kiss her passionately. She tried with all her might to resist him but failed miserably. Karly kissed him back while muttering "I hate you so much Jamal'. Oh yeah well let's see this hatred for me Karly, Jamal said carefully laying her on the bed. He began to take off her shirt while kissing her from her neck to her breasts. Karly is moaning because her body truly yearned for this, but her mind kept going back to catching him cheating. Before she realized they were naked in her mother's house. Jamal was inside of her, and she was loving every bit of him. Jamal wasn't built like a normal guy he had a monster package. Karly hadn't had sex since the last time she was with him, so she really felt him when he penetrated her. Ummmm, she moaned as he whispered in her ear "turn around baby". Karly was then under Jamal's spell once again. She had gone from laying on her back to being up on her knees with her face down and ass up. Jamal stroked her whining his hips left to right and right to left deeper and deeper. Karly moaned louder and louder as she gripped the sheets while biting the pillow. Jamal wasn't done with her yet, he then flipped her like a pancake and pinned her up on the wall. Karly was dripping wet all over him as both worked up a serious sweat. Karly felt her vagina stretching with every stroke Jamal gave.

 The closer he got to reaching his peak, the weaker Jamal became. Karly then pushed him to the bed as she climbed on and took him for a hell of a ride, now he's moaning and groaning gripping her ass bouncing her up and down faster and faster until he exploded all

42

inside of her. This was the first time Jamal hadn't used protection their entire relationship. Karly too had exploded all over him at the same exact time. This was no ordinary feeling to her, and she was definitely going to have a new walk for a few days. Karly, I truly love you, I'm just ready to settle down Jamal spoke sincerely. Jamal don't ruin a perfectly good sex session with this bullshit Karly responded. Karly it's not like that I just need you to know that I do truly love you with everything in me, it's just not time for us right now and I'm sorry for everything I've done that hurt you.... can you forgive me? Jamal asked patiently awaiting a response from Karly as they both got dressed. Instead, Karly sat there trying hard not to break down and cry because all she heard was, she was losing the only male who ever showed real signs of caring for her. So, she let out a deep sigh which sounded like a sigh of relief to Jamal causing him to feel a little on edge since he knew Karly felt the same way about him. With nothing else spoken from the two they got up and walked back down the stairs to the living room to finish watching television.

    ALICE CLOSE THE DOOR!!! Chandra shouted as she walked up to the front door. Hey Jamal, Karly can you help me get the bags from the car Chandra said gently. Ok mom Karly stated as she got up as slow as possible thinking to herself (Damn I'm sore as shit) walking out towards the car Jamal followed so Chandra wouldn't notice Karly and the way she was moving at that moment. I don't need your help Jamal Karly said rudely you aren't my man remember taunting him. As a matter of fact, you can take your ass home and get away from me for good this time. Jamal stands there stuck as if he missed something, looking at

43

    Karly trying to figure out why she seems to have so much hatred in her eyes as they stand their face to face. Karly I'm still your friend and nothing is going to change that Jamal said quietly. Well friend you can go home or wherever but just get out of my face and good luck with the rest of your life nonchalantly Karly spoke. Jamal just walked off and got into his car leaving not even looking back at Karly as he drove away. Karly finished getting the things from the car her mom asked her to get and went into the house closing and locking the door behind her. Mom I'm going up to my room if you need me said Karly. Wow what a day Karly thought, as she laid across her bed listening to music doodling in her journal thinking about her life in a whole new aspect. She knew one thing if she didn't know anything else and that was, she and Jamal were definitely through especially with him leaving for the army. Karly pulled out her phone book and called Rashad to see how he was feeling. They hadn't talked since the incident between him and Jamal. Rashad had moved back to the city and went back into the thuggish lifestyle telling Karly how everything was going for him.

    Karly just sat and listened wishing she was up there where all the excitement was instead of being down in the country bored. Rashad had told her he would be down the middle of next year, but they could talk everyday if she wanted. That was the close of one chapter and the opening of a whole chapter of Karly's life. As months and months went by Karly and Rashad talked daily as promised learning more and more about one another as time passed. Rashad began to have stronger feelings for Karly, and she started to develop feelings for him as well. Although they were many of miles apart Rashad couldn't help but wondering how it would feel to hold Karly in his arms as more than friends. Though he never spoke in any other type of way towards Karly she knew he was starting to want more than a friendship. The thing was Karly wasn't looking for anything more than a friend. She was about to turn another year older, and it was her time to just enjoy being a teenager. Karly knew she just wanted to make it through high school and leave that town. She continued to attend school, work and play sports she barely had time to do anything. She still talked to Rashad but not as much as before with everything she had going on now. Karly's birthday was around the corner, and she had no clue what she was getting into, but she knew she was going to have fun since she was off the entire weekend.

Chanelle her best friend had plans for them to get into something but never told Karly what it was. A lot of time had passed since her and Jamal had split for good, so she hadn't had sex with anybody in almost two years. Karly thought to herself it sure would be nice to have sex for her birthday but didn't spend a long time entertaining the thought all she knew was she was turning another year older, and she was going to enjoy it. "Mom" Karly said as she made her way down the stairs, I'm off to get my hair and nails done for tonight I will call you later to let you know what's up love ya and out the door she went. Chanelle was just pulling up at Karly's house to start their day celebrating her birthday. As they are riding through town Karly's cell phone rings and it's a local number, she doesn't know so she didn't answer it. "Nell girl what's on the agenda for today after our hair and nail appointment" Karly asks? Shit girl you know I got some good shit planned for your ass Channel responded as they both giggled. Pulling

45

up to the hair salon they both exit the car and as Karly looked up there Jamal stood fine as hell. Karly dropped her head and cut her eye at Chanelle she had on a baseball cap a nice pair of jeans with a cute blue tee shirt to match. She wasn't dressed to see anybody at the moment she was just trying to get her hair and nails done. Approaching the door to the salon she spoke to everybody out there but Jamal. Karly was pissed at Chanelle because she knew nobody, but Chanelle could have told him where she would be. Hey, the birthday girl has arrived to get all sexy for her special day Janice stated. Hey girl Karly responded.......

    Oh, wait a minute little mama what's wrong? You're not about to be sounding like that going into your birthday weekend Janice boldly stated. I'm good Ms. Janice just thinking that's all softly Karly spoke. As time went by Chanelle and Karly both sat in the chair as Janice and Kelly transformed them into two totally different females. Chanelle had been engaged in the conversation that had been going on all around her as Karly sat quietly wondering what her day was going to be like since it had been damn near two years since she laid eyes on Jamal. She knew she had gotten over him but couldn't understand why her stomach felt as though it was in knots since she saw him outside as they were coming into the salon. Just as she went into deep thought the door came open and a strong smell of cologne seemed to be getting closer. Karly looked up and there stood Jamal smiling as if they were still together and had been for a while. Karly seemed to be confused but she didn't show it.

    WHAT JAMAL? Karly said rudely. "Now Karly I know your momma taught you better than that "Janice stated. Sorry Ms. Janice I apologize

for my attitude I'm just not in the mood for any dumb stuff it's my birthday. Yes, darling I know that too, but you have to talk to people the way you would like them to talk to you keep that in mind. Yes Ma'am Ms. Janice. Karly, do you have a minute, Jamal spoke sincerely. Sigh...... I guess so Karly answered. She had just a few minutes until Chanelle was done in the chair, so she walked outside with Jamal to see what he wanted. Once outside Jamal had something to tell Karly but didn't know how to say it. Jamal, I don't have all day what do you want with me? Karly stated arrogantly. Karly, I wanted you to be the first to know I have a son and another child on the way Jamal quickly said and I wanted you to be the first to know before anybody else told you. Tears filled Karly's eyes as she turned away from Jamal and said "ok thanks for sharing, congratulations" as she walked away as fast as she could.

    Once back inside the salon tears just ran out her eyes uncontrollably. She asked Kelly how much longer it would be with

Channel. I will be done in about a half hour Kelly stated turning to face Karly quickly noticing she's crying. Oh my god baby what's wrong do I need to call Chandra? Kelly asked. No no ma'am I'm ok just tears of joy. Chanelle turned around and said Karly I've known you damn near your whole life those are far from tears of joy luv what's up? He went and had kids Nell!!! Karly shouted WHAT!!!!! Janice, Kelly, and Chanelle shouted....... And he decided to tell you on your fucking birthday Janice stated....... Hell, nawl you don't do no shit like that!!!...... Everybody in the salon went from being happy to being pissed in about five seconds. My whole birthday is shot y'all how am I going to enjoy myself when my heart hurts? Karly sadly spoke.

47

 The salon became quiet, nobody knew what to say to Karly however everyone knew how she felt. They all have been heartbroken a time or two, so they shared her sadness. All right enough of that sad shit let's brighten up the mood Chanelle said as she got up and cut on the music. Let's get this party started early ladies since we all are celebrating Karly's birthday together later anyway…… Yes, let's do that Kelly responded.

 Karly what are you wearing this evening Janice asked? Well Ms. Janice I was going to just dress up a pair of jeans but now I feel like I want to be even sexier. Go ahead girl it's your birthday you can wear whatever the hell you want Kelly laughed. Nell, I thought you said you had a surprise for me girl Karly stated in a brighter mood. I do mama just not yet, wait until night fall and you'll see what I have in store strictly for you Chanelle said anxiously. She couldn't wait to see the look on Karly's face when she seen just who her surprise was. Welp ladies it's been real but birthday girl and I have to go get our outfits for this evening so we will catch you gals later on Chanelle said as her and Karly walked out the salon on their way shopping.

    Once in the car Karly sat there as quiet as a mouse with all sorts of shit running through her mind. Chanelle asked Karly what made Jamal want to tell her about his kid and one on the way. Karly let out a sigh and stated he claimed he didn't want me to hear it from anybody else but him. Damn!!! Chanelle just shook her head as they began riding to the mall continuing their girl's day out. Oh, shit let me call mom Karly remembered........ "Hello, hey mom it's me Nell and I are on our way to the mall, do you need anything before we leave town?" Karly asked her mother, as her and Chanelle made their way through

town. "No Karly we are just fine, you just be careful and have fun baby".... Ok mom I will as she hung up her cell. Shit Nel off to the mall girl let's go see what niggas out shopping today who are looking for young independent ladies who are just trying to be friends said Karly. Yes, girl I'm down with that Channel responded as the two prepared themselves for the long ride to the mall.

Karly and Channel rode and laughed all the way to the mall preparing themselves for a lovely evening of partying. Ring ring ring....... ring ring ring....... Karly's phone started going once again. "Damn Karly your shit blowing up today isn't it" Channel said. I don't know what for Karly responded I don't feel like being bothered with nobody from my past as she pressed the ignore button placing her phone back in her purse. Oh yeah well what about Rashad Channel said as she dug for information. Come on Nell it's not like that between Rashad and I Karly defending herself. Even though she had thought about what it would be like to be intimate with Rashad that was none of Channel's business. "Okay girl you don't have to convince me of shit all I'm saying is I know you've thought about what was in that niggas pants though as fine as he is" Nel said. Girl you're a damn mess ha ha ha ha Karly giggled as they walked on into the mall.

    Oh my God.......... "Karly, do you see those niggas up there standing in front of the Footlocker" Channel noticed as soon as they entered the mall. Girl I'm not worried about that right now I got enough nigga problems I don't need any new ones chuckled Karly. Girl please ain't no harm in looking, girl damn......... Chanelle stated. The two continue through the mall looking for the right kind of outfit for later in the evening. Laughing, joking, and enjoying themselves while shopping was

totally mind consuming so Karly had no time to think about the shit going on between her and Jamal. However, from that day forth it will always be like a plague in her mind. Karly loved Jamal but deep down she knew things between them would never be the same. Starring off in space lost in her thoughts she didn't notice the mixed looking guy walking towards her. "Umm excuse Miss" he spoke in her ear with a sexy erotic voice.

    Karly turned slowly trying to not seem amazed, softly speaking "my name is Karly". What's up my name is Jason, but my friends call me Jay for short, the young man stated. Karly and Chanelle couldn't help but noticed how sexy Jason was standing about six-foot four caramel complected with a muscle shirt on showing his entire build, and deep waves in is fresh cut. Karly thought damn I gotta tell this one about the birthday bash their throwing me tonight, and right before she could get it out Channel blabbed it out of her mouth. Hey Jay, we are throwing my girl Karly a huge birthday bash tonight on the southeast side of town you and your sexy friends should come check it out excitingly Channel spoke. "Oh word, Karly it's your birthday huh?" .... Jason responded. "Yes, it's my birthday bash you should come check it out if your girlfriend doesn't have plans for y'all" Karly said annoyingly. "Shawtie I'm single and free to mingle if you catch what I'm saying Jason responded quickly". Channel cheesing while Karly fought back blushing, they both cut their eyes at one another while saying "heyyyyyyy"!!!! Jason and Karly exchanged numbers and off they went each looking back to see if the group of guys were watching them walk away.

Damn!!!!!!! Karly girl you on fire today ain't you Channel teasing Karly as they finished up their shopping for the party. Shit girl you know I gotta be on my shit tonight, it's going to be so many sexy ass niggas in that place tonight I better get me a piece Karly stated seriously and they both laughed. Channel had her outfit together they were still working on Karly's as Channel's cell phone rang as she looked up at Karly and "said girl this nigga has got to be playing games when he knows we ain't spoke in over six months. I wonder what the hell he wants, I bet you it's dealing with your party tonight." Nell go ahead and handle that I will finish getting my shit tight for tonight and I'll meet you over by the wishing well, Karly told

Chanelle. "Ok girl take your time I ain't going nowhere this nigga fitting to try to talk his way into the party just to see me watch what I tell you" Chanelle stated laughing as she exits the store.

    That damn girl is a fool Karly mumbled to herself, while finalizing her outfit for her party, after all she had to be the sexiest bitch in the spot since it was all about her. Walking out the store Karly gets bumped by this pregnant female who she has never seen before, so of course she brushed it off thinking it was just crowded and she was wobbling since she was so big. Reaching into her purse searching for her phone Karly noticed Chanelle talking to another group of dudes and slowed her pace down at least until they walked away. She didn't feel like flirting anymore at this moment she had to save a little of it for the party. It seemed like it was taking Chanelle long enough to get rid of the dudes so Karly sat at a distance where she could see her. Nell noticed Karly and smiled while Karly just shook her head. While she

51

had her phone out she decided to check to make sure she didn't miss no calls or receive any text messages. Damn!!!! Karly said quietly to herself she had nine missed calls and fifteen texts. Once she opened them up, she started to get angry. (Why the hell is this nigga calling and texting me like he is losing his damn mind) Karly thought to herself I wonder what this is all about. She texts him back to find out what the hell he wanted. "JAMAL WHAT THE HELL DO YOU WANT!!!" she texted back.......

"KARLY, WE NEED TO TALK, BABY IT'S IMPORTANT I KNOW I FUCKED UP BIG TIME PLEASE ALLOW ME TO EXPLAIN" .... Karly closes her phone and throws it into her purse as she walks up to Channel, "Nell we gotta go girl now" Karly what's wrong? Chanelle said with worry in her voice. I'll show you when we get to the car girl Karly shouted. Speed walking to the car they get outside, and Karly looks up and there the same pregnant girl from the store is leaning on Chanelle's car. "BITCH, what the fuck are you doing on my car" Chanelle yelled at the pregnant chick. Oh, this is your car the pregnant girl said Well allow me to introduce myself, I'm Kia and I want to know which one of you bitches is fucking with my baby daddy. "BABYDADDY" HAHAHAHAHA Karly and Channel both started laughing because they weren't for the bullshit. Both Channel and Karly were well known for fighting and everybody knew they could and would fight together if it ever came down to it. They both knew if they whipped this pregnant girl's as they would be arrested. So, with her blood boiling deep down inside of her Karly knew this had to be the bitch Jamal had gotten pregnant while he was away enlisted in the army. What she couldn't figure out was why this bitch was out here all alone starting shit she wasn't really ready to deal with. Even though Karly loved Jamal she

wasn't about to let her day be ruined so she tried to walk away until Kia spit on her. "Bitch I know you didn't just spit on me" Karly yelled while swinging and punching Kia directly in her damn face.

"Karly"!!!! Chanelle screamed she's pregnant....... Karly continued to hit Kia not caring where her hits landed while Chanelle tried to pull her away and push her into the car. Once Karly had come back around and realized Kia was lying in the parking lot bleeding from her face, she became afraid for the baby, so she pulled out her phone and called Jamal. "Hello...... Umm yeah you might want to get to the parking lot of the mall and get your bitch" Karly stated in a nonchalantly. "Hello what the fuck do you mean Karly, bitch what did you do to my baby mama?" Jamal said frantically. HaHaHa, I rearranged that bitch face for spitting on me that's what the fuck I did to your baby mama nigga and lose my fucking number before the same damn thing happens to your bitch ass, Karly said hysterically while wiping Kia's blood from her hands.

Nell girl that shit felt good as hell to just whip that bitch like that, well chick I hope you ready for war because you know Jamal and whomever that girl's people are going to want to wreck Channel stated calmly as possible. Karly just sat back and thought about how a Jamal could run to the aid of a bitch he barely knew and have treated her like shit since he took her virginity. As the two continued riding back to their houses to get ready for Karly's party Nell told her she wasn't going to be the one to pick her up. Karly was ordered to be dressed by eight because someone incredibly special and dear to her was picking her up. Oh, okay so that's how you going to do now huh, I'm supposed to be your girl Karly teased. Oh, girl be quiet and just be on your best shit tonight Nell blushed while pulling up to Karly's house.

53

    Alright girl, I'll see you at the party ladybug, no doubt Karly replied as she exited Nel's whip. Karly approached her house and noticed her mom's car was gone and all the lights were out, so she was going to be home alone. This is the best way to get dressed without any Hassel she thought as she entered her house. It was 6pm on the dot and she had two hours to turn herself from beautiful to gorgeous. She put in her favorite slow jam cd thinking about who she would love to feel deep inside of her since it was her birthday. Little did she know her night was going to be one she wouldn't ever forget for as long as she lived. Once in the house Karly headed straight to her room to start preparing for her birthday celebration.

Clothes laid out on the bed, bath water running and the soft tunes jumping on the radio. While in the bathtub Karly sat and thought about how she would like her night to go, and whom she would love to leave the party with. Deep in thought Karly began to massage her nipples as they grew hard and pointy as if they were being sucked on. Ummm Rashad would be a nice, lovely surprise for me to leave the party with and even allow him to penetrate her deep, Karly thought to herself and couldn't help but to reach down in between her legs to run her fingers over her clit as it throbbed for some serious attention. Damn she thought to herself I hope Nell has some rubbers because I've not had any use for them here lately so I'm all out............... Losing herself once again in deep sexual thoughts about Rashad, she then realized it was just about time for her ride to be pulling up any minute. At least by that time her makeup was flawless, and she smelt really good all that was left for her to do was slide her outfit she and Nell picked out earlier that day on and she was ready to party. Karly did her famous twirl in her body mirror and

out the room down the stairs she went. Car lights shined through the windows of her living room and out the door she started "see ya later mom I'm on my way to the party" Karly shouted. Okay sweetie be careful and call me if you need me Chandra replied as Karly shut the door. Damn she said as she looked at the stretch Navigator limo that had pulled up in her yard. Karly took her time and slowly walked to the limo wondering who the hell was in it, and why Nell hadn't told her exactly who was picking her up. The closer she got to the limo the more her heart pounded from the expense and excitement. Karly loved mysteries however she didn't like it when people kept her in the dark about anything. The door opens to the limo as Karly got right up beside the front making her way to the back, she goes to turn around and notice her mom standing out on the front step smiling as if she already knew who was in the limo sent to pick up her daughter. When Karly turned back to the limo, she was speechless. She couldn't believe her eyes it was the sexiest brother she had ever seen…….

Chapter 6

OH MY GOD RASHAD, is it really you boo? Karly screamed to the top of her lungs. She jumped up and down like a big baby as tears started to run down her face. Aww baby girl doesn't cry Rashad said as he wiped Karly's makeup from running. Boo I've not seen you since all that shit went down and you were released from the hospital, Karly stated so shockingly. Yea baby girl I know I had a lot of things I had to take care of, and it was time for me to make something out of my life, so I stayed away. All you had to do was call me Karly I always thought about you and asked about you when I talked to my people. Come on get in we have a party to attend and you're the guest of honor Rashad smiled as he took Karly's hand and escorted her into the limo. Karly heart skipped two beats it felt like when Rashad grabbed her hand and touched her back. Damn I wanted to see him, now I can't seem to pull myself together around him Karly thought. Once in the limo Karly and Rashad just talked and laughed all the way to the party. They suddenly got quiet as Rashad told Karly this was just the beginning of her gifts that she would be receiving that evening. Umm what are you some kind of boss now Karly joked with Rashad. No baby girl my business is just doing really well that's all, and besides you know if I could, I would give you the entire world in the palm of your hands Rashad said quietly to Karly. Karly sat and blushed a little while looking up through the sunroof at the star lit night while riding on their way to the party. Rashad noticed her mellow demeanor and hollered through the intercom to the driver "yo Steve man hook us up with the jams man." Karly noticed the ride became a bit longer than she assumed it would, so she started to wonder what Rashad had

planned for her as the lights became dim and the music played really soft. Karly knew she wanted Rashad from day one when she met him, and although they were the best of friends, she couldn't allow herself to fall for him. "Damn he smells so good, and the way he is looking right now is driving me crazy" Karly get it together she thought to herself. So shorty what would you like to do tonight Rashad asked Karly as the soft music played in the background. What do you mean Karly responded you know I'm having a party and I'm the guest of honor, so I have to be there... "Yeah yeah yeah, I already know this Karly I was just playing with you girl" Rashad said jokingly. Sir we will be arriving at the party in less than two minutes the driver stated as they sat and laughed in the back. Rashad, Karly said softly I really appreciate your friendship over the years and how you've been able to just be my friend and not disrespecting me in any way. She then leaned in and kissed him on the cheek whispering thank you. Rashad knew just by what Karly said and the way she said it that she obviously felt the same way he felt but he just smiled and got out the limo, walking around to open her door and they both approach the party.

    Hey Karly, Rashad said softly tonight is your night baby girl and I want you to enjoy it. I'll be here all night so if you need a ride home baby girl, I'll take you just to make sure you get home safely without any dumb stuff. Aww thanks Rashad Karly hugs him tightly as they enter the building. SURPRISE!!!!!!! Everyone screams as Rashad opens the door while Karly walks in. Karly didn't know who to approach first because it was just so many friends and family members there, she just made her way around the room as the night progressed. This was truly going to be a night Karly would definitely remember. Music playing loads of food the most gorgeous guy in the building wanting to be mines, God my night can't possibly get any better Karly was thinking. Wonder how tonight will end up Karly thought as she sat at the table watching Rashad maneuver his way around the room. Damn I wonder how his body moves between those sheets Karly went off into a sexual fantasy daydreaming about her best male friend. Karly...... Karly.... KARLY!!!! Nell shouted while trying to snap her out of her fantasy damn girl what the hell got you so lost in here tonight..., Rashad that's who got me a bit clueless right now chick. Any who Karly said while shaking herself back to reality, what's popping Nell? Girl all these sexy ass niggas in here and you asking me what's popping, shit I'm about to shake my ass on one of these dudes in here Nell stated as the two girls walked around the party peeping the scene, while doing so Nell notices a group of niggas standing in the corner watching Rashad. Those dudes had been watching him since they arrived, and Karly had noticed too. Nell I'm about to make my way over to Rashad and see what's actually on the agenda for tonight after the party, keep an eye on those clowns over there in the corner because them niggas look like they're up to no fucken good. Karly girl I'm already on that shit mama go handle your business with "your boo" Nell teased. As she walked across the dance floor Rashad noticed her coming and he actually got up and met her halfway. Hours had passed since they got to the party and the building had to be cleaned once everyone had left so Karly just wanted to know if she really had Rashad for the rest of the evening as he stated earlier. So beautiful what's on your mind? Karly stood there a bit puzzled trying to figure

60

Out how the hell he knew she had something on her mind. Well, I was just wondering what you had to do after my party because I know you're a busy young man, Karly stated in a nonchalant type of manner. Baby girl I'm waiting on you to tell me when you're ready to bounce, my presence at this party was strictly for you Rashad replied. Well, let me find Nell and see what she ready to do because mom and my aunts are planning to clean up the building so she told me I can go ahead and leave whenever I was ready said Karly as she walked away switching her ass enough for Rashad to bite his lip and shake his head. Damn boss one of Rashad's employees shouted shawty make me wanna dig all up in her just by the way she walks. "Man, what the fuck you say?" replied Rashad as he grabbed the nigga by the throat. You better not never let me hear you come out your mouth like that ever again or it will be the last thing you ever utter nigga threatened Rashad as he shoved the nigga away from him. Yo Tony which was the right hand of Tony man we ready to split before I fuck this nigga up in here and I don't wanna ruin baby girls evening shattering this niggas blood Rashad stated. Ok homeboy let me tell this chick we ready to bounce said Tony. Oh, shit my nigga you don't ever holla at chicks who is this chick I wanna meet her replied Rashad. Let me see if I can find her homie and you sure will meet her Tony said jokingly. Tony walks away and walks towards where Karly and Nell were standing and outs his arms around Nell and she brightened right up as he kisses her on the neck excuse me baby but my mans wants to meet you, remember the one I had been telling you is like my little brother Tony whispered to Nell in her ear. Oh, shit ok boop come on girl his little brother is the one I told you that you should let me introduce you to Nell replied to

61

Karly excitingly. Oh, here the hell we go Karly is thinking but being the friend, she is she walks on over there with Nell. She notices that they are walking in the direction Rashad was in and the last thing she wanted was a strange ass dude pushing up on her in front of him. Oh man are you kidding me Tony you seeing my baby girl's best friend Nell???? Rashad shouted oh my nigga she is real good people's. Wait my dude how the fuck you know my baby Tony replied angerly. Oh man chill that's Karly best friend said Rashad. OH SHIT!!!! Are you serious so all those times you said you would call me back Nell because you were with your home girl Karly? Tony responded puzzled. Ah yes honey Nell said laughing so hard. Oh my God if y'all could see your faces Nell said looking at Rashad and Karly. Karly we've been talking for about two years now and been wanting you guys to meet but had no clue it would be you and Rashad meeting. Nell said laughing hysterically. Damn dog you were planning on hooking me up with somebody all this time and never knew it was my baby girl, wow Rashad said. Karly still standing there stuck but laughing as well because she couldn't believe it herself. Well since all this is now out the way how about we all go take a ride and finish the rest of our evening just chilling Rashad suggested. Sure, let's go I'm with it everyone agreed. Let me go kiss my momma and tell her I'll see her in the morning in case we up and do something crazy like leave town tonight Karly stated I'll meet y'all outside. AS everyone is starting towards the door Nell notices a couple of people moving really quickly towards the door and points it out to Tony, who signals Rashad and they both slow down and start looking around to see what else they see around the building since the both of them have been in similar situations up in the city. Nell goes and finds Karly and her mom making sure they were ok. They were in the kitchen putting food together and talking about where Karly was going and who she was going with. Nell comes in and starts to help put the food away and pack plates with Karly and her mom when Karly gives her a puzzling look like what the hell are you doing in here......? Nell says to Karly the boys had to do something really quick, so I came in here thinking she didn't want to startle Karly or anyone else for that matter. Meanwhile Rashad and Tony realized it was nothing serious going on so they paged Nell and Karly so that they could go on about the rest of their night as planned.

Chapter 7

Damn I want some dick Karly thought to herself while sipping on the shot of Grey Goose Rashad had fixed from the open bar in the back of the limo. Glancing over there only to see Tony's hands all over Nell as she giggled and squirmed. So, what's on your mind Rashad leaned over and whispered to Karly intimately. Some alone time with you would be nice, uttered Karly with a real mysterious look in her eyes. Driver a yo Driver Rashad shouted through the intercom can you take us to the cabin please thanks. Karly's heart started to beat really fast Oh my God did he say the cabin??? Shit I best get on my big girl shit because this is a certified grown ass man, I'm with tonight. Yet again looking in Nell's direction hoping she would glance over so she could make sure all was well with her and the plan to end up at the cabin. Baby girl I want you to sit back and relax we will be arriving at the cabin shortly, Rashad smiled as he caressed Karly's neck. Damn that shit feels so good, I can only imagine what he has in store for me tonight, after all it is my birthday Karly smiled. While Karly and Rashad, we are caressing one another the driver announced over the intercom we would be arriving at the cabin in about 5-10 minutes. Oh shit, Karly thought to herself....... Now is the time I must prove myself and not be afraid to take it there with Rashad. The limo comes to a complete holt and the time has come to be alone with Rashad. Karly is more than anxious but at the same time she is extremely nervous. Baby girl this is your night what would you like to do first, it is your birthday Rashad stated. Yessssss that's right Chanelle replied, as they all exited the limo heading towards the cabin. Getting to the door Tony asked for everyone to hold on as he reached in his pocket to grab the keys so everyone could get in. Once in the cabin the girls realized both Tony and Rashad had already been to the cabin prior to the ladies to set it up with all the birthday celebration supplies. Oh my gosh Rashad you really set this place up like another party was going to take place here or something. So, I take it that you like the way we prepared the place for you guys huh, replied to Rashad. Like it...., baby I love it thank you so much Karly shouted while hugging and kissing on Rashad. Well man I don't know what you two are about to get yourselves into, but Nell and I are about to go upstairs and do what we do. Nell you straight Karly asked.... "Yeah, boo I'm good I have condoms and everything else I could possibly need to enjoy the rest of my night" replied Nell. Cool I'll see your ass in the morning girl, Karly responded as Nell and Tony disappeared to their room for the evening. As Karly turned around, she noticed Rashad had put on some slow music and lit the candles, he started to approach her as she fiddled with her hair. Karly I've been wanting this time with you ever since our date at the movies got ruined. Aww baby I see that now, so what would you like to get into now that you have me alone Karly seductively asked while biting her lip. Rashad grabbed her softly behind her neck and kissed passionately as he began to run his hands all over her body. He picked her up and placed her on the mantle and unfastened her blouse, as her voluptuous breast peaked out from her blouse. The kissing became more intense as they both start peeling one another's clothes off, hearts racing, moans and groans are filling the air Rashad reaches over to grab protection, but Karly stops him and say I trust you .... With a serious stare into one another's eyes at that moment they both knew what the outcome could be taking such a risk but neither cared.

65

Rashad enters Karly and she lets out a loud but sexy gasp for air, thinking to herself it's time to experience just what Rashad has been trying to give her all along. She wraps her legs around him and pushes him deeper into her, he's moaning she's groaning their bodies are swaying together as the slow jams play in the background. He then takes her down from the mantle and bends her over while he enters her from the back. Karly is pushing back while Rashad is stroking her all she could think about was damn this negro feels amazing. She has never had a guy take his time like this with her making sure he is touching every single spot and causing her to cum numerous times. She has now found herself on her back laying on a Persian rug in front of the fireplace, bodies glistening and still making love. Karly had no clue how much more of him her frame could handle but she damn sure wasn't about to throw in the towel just yet...... She flips him over so that now she is on top, and she is grinding on his dick as he caresses her breast and even sits up to put each of them in his mouth. Karly feels herself about to cum again, only this time Rashad is pumping a little bit faster than earlier and before she could even say baby, I'm about to cum Rashad said damn girl I'm about to....... And they both came at the same damn time. OH MY GOD!!!!!! Baby what in the hell did we just do, Karly questioned with a drained look on her face. Rashad with a drained but exhausted voice replied and said we just made love baby girl that's what we just did, and it was awesome you felt so damn good. Why thank you boo, you felt amazing as well. The two laid there while cuddling until they both fell asleep. Boom boom boom boom boom a loud knock comes on the door Rashad hops up and tony comes running down the stairs WHAT THE FUCK IS THAT MAN.... Tony shouts. Man, I don't fucking know but you got the strap, asked Rashad ...

Damn right I got the strap homie, you know Tony stay strapped at all times just for situations like this one my dude. Baby girl you and ya homegirl go over there behind the bar and stay down, instructed Rashad. Both Karly and Chanelle went and hid as they were told. Oh, shit man what the fuck!!!!! Oh my god Nell that sounded like Rashad, where the hell is Tony??? Shhhh Shhhh I'm going to try to peep around the corner and see if I can get a glance at what the hell is going on, whispered Nell. Ok Ok Ok Karly responded. Karly girl you're not even going to believe this, look let me show you Nell said. Karly peeps around the corner and Chanelle has a gun in her face, bitch get the fuck up...... Wait what Chanelle what's going on, Karly uttered. Bitch we are robbing this motherfucker that's what's going the fuck on. Baby, bring that little bitch over here with this coward ass. Damn Nell it's like that now chick, you've been my ace for many of years and now, over some dick you going to turn your back on me and agree to this shit, shouted Karly. Bitch please this is business, fuck all that bullshit you spitting, Nell responded. Tony boo where are we going to put them, Chanelle asked? Oh, I have a plan for the both of them smirked Tony. Karly with tears in her eyes looked over to see the same exact guys who came up in her party sitting to the dining room table counting money with Tony and Rashad lying unconscious on the floor. Oh, shit is what went through Karly's mind, how the hell am I going to get out of this? With Rashad laying over there, I don't stand a chance of surviving this crap unless I can convince Nell to talk to Tony about letting me go. Nell, Karly yelled angrily I have to go to the restroom, Nell looked at Tony who snared and said go ahead and take that whore to the restroom if she tries anything, kill her.... Nell's response was gladly. Damn Karly thought this bitch is really down for this nigga....

67

Shit this is a chick I grew up with, and she is willing to kill me over some dick and money......How the hell can I get out of this? As they approached the bathroom Karly noticed Chanelle had put the gun in the back of her pants so her hands are free, so it was either now or never so Karly swung as hard as she could and hit Nell in her face. The girls wrestled, and rolled all around upstairs, Tony sends one of his goons up there to see what the hell is going on and when he gets to the top of the stairs, he sees the girls fighting. He immediately snatched Karly up and allowed Chanelle to get up and adjust herself after slapping Karly across the face with her 9mm pistol, fracturing her jaw. Now bitch the next time you try that shit, I'm going to have them kill you and your family laughed Nell. Come on bitch said the man to Karly as he escorts her down the stairs. While going downstairs Karly realized Rashad wasn't anywhere in the area, she seen him in before she went upstairs. The closer she got to the living room she looked over to see Rashad tied up at the kitchen table while tony is shouting in his face. All she could hear was Rashad moaning and groaning as Tony and his goons are torturing him trying to get the answers they want about his fortune. Stop it y'all are going to beat him to death, then how the hell will you ever learn where his money is shouted Chanelle. Ok!!! FINE Tony responded, kneeling down in Rashad's face you're going to take me to your money, or you'll die sooner than you think bruh whispered tony. GET HIS ASS UP YO!!! Tony yelled, come on motherfucker let's take a ride. Wait what the hell do we do with her Chanelle yelled, oh yea this little sexy ass bitch Tony smiled. Hey Ray and Mike, y'all keep Karly company here at the cabin and once this motherfucker gives me access to the funds, I'll call y'all and that's when

you guys let that bitch go. After all my beef ain't never been with her, she cool people for real. Tony then kneeled down and looked Karly in her face and said I hope it's no hard feeling Lil Mama, laughing as he walked on out the cabin with Chanelle on his arm. Karly sat there with the most frightening look on her face at this point because she had no clue what these guys were about or even if they were going to really let her go. Sitting in the corner sobbing hysterically one of the guys said Hey lil mama it's going to be ok, you're going to be out of here in no time. The other guy laughed out loudly saying yeah, she will but she going to have to put in some work to be able to do that……….

Chapter 8

As the sun gleamed in from the side of the windows Chandra looks as if she has no hope in learning what has happened to her daughter and her daughter friend. She's called everybody and has made countless phone calls to both Karly and Chanelle's cellphones. She is about ready to take matters in her own hands. Drastically seeking help from their neighborhood and law enforcement figures, yet it's not lead them any closer to knowing the whereabouts of the girls. It's been months now and Chandra has been taking private investigation classes and working at the production plant keeping close watch on the younger two children when they are out in about. She is truly determined to find her girls by any means necessary. One day while in the grocery store a young man who looked as if she had seen him somewhere before caught her eye. It was something about his that sent chills down Chandra's spine. Going through what she is going through she tried not to make everyone a suspect, even though her gut was telling her that something about this young man wasn't right. With that in mind Chandra got behind him in line, she wasn't trying to cause any type of attention so she acted as normal as she could. The young man's turn came up as he placed his items on the belt, Chandra noticed he had a lot of things she would buy for young adults, however he didn't as if he even liked some of those things he was purchasing. This may sound weird but a lot of food matches people's personalities, Chandra thought to herself. Once the man had paid for his groceries, he then left the store. He was a neatly looking young man and seemed to have manners, yet Chandra really felt some kind of connection with him, and it didn't set well with her. Once home Chandra tried to shake

that encounter with the gentleman at the store by doing everything she could possibly do. The younger two children of hers would help around the house and keep her laughing at their goofiness which kept her entertained as much as they could. Both of the kids knew if they didn't step up and be there for their mom she would fall completely apart. After all it had been almost 6 months since they had seen or spoken to their sister, and their mother is all they have keeping her on her toes is a Must.... Got damn it, why is it taking them so long to release me to my family, Karly thought to herself while Tony's dude sat and watch the game. I've not heard from Rashad, Tony or Nell I have no clue if Rashad is even still alive. I just wish I could hear his voice and hear him tell me its ok baby girl I'm fine. Even after being here at this beautiful cabin for months, it still all feels like a bogus ass dream to me. Getting up going to what she has now made into her bedroom falling on her bed she knew she has to find some way the hell up out of there before these guys began to get restless. So far, they've not tried anything with her, however the way they looked at her is what made her feel very uncomfortable and even more certain that she had to come up with something and quickly. KNOCK KNOCK KNOCK KNOCK....... Karly awakened from what she thought was just a quiet cozy little nap to a series of knocks on her door, which she kept locked at all times. Who is it she yelled, come on open the door girl and stop playing? Karly gets up and opens the door and it's Mike bringing up her dinner and Ray not far behind making sure she was still there and hadn't escaped. Damn did you have to knock so fucking loud Karly snared. Sorry lil mama I tried to knock softly but you didn't answer responded Mike. Mike was the one whom I could tell was soft and gentle, he really never even looked at me as a piece of meat, not like Ray looked at me. I kind of feel a little more relaxed when Mike is around because I don't think he'd allow Ray to do anything to me. That's probably why Mike allows Ray to do the grocery shopping so I could get a little relief while he is away from the cabin. Karly realizing that Mike is probably her best chance of getting out of there she soon devises a plan. The first thing I'm going to need is a weapon, something that will back these motherfuckers off of me should the time present itself. Karly than began to look around the cabin every chance she got in search for something she could use for a weapon and was easily to hide. All she could think about was getting away from there and couldn't help but wonder what has happened to Rashad. Mike and Ray knew Karly was an intelligent individual so when they spoke about the situation they almost always stepped out on the porch. As another moon crept out Karly has stepped into the schedule, she created for herself since she's been held captive. The night was no different the guys were watching the sports channel, and she was up in her bedroom watching television while writing in a book, her mind wondering off about all sorts of things but mainly what she was going to do when she got up out this mess. Dozing off Karly hears a loud thump and a bunch of arguing, so like any other chick she went to go see what the hell was going on and why the hell the guys were making such a loud ass ruckus. As she started for the stars, she heard Mike and Ray arguing and a bunch of heavy breathing. Mike was trying to damn near kill Ray for joking around about doing some kind of harm to her, so she then decided she was going to watch Mike whip Ray's ass as if she was in an arena watching Tyson and Holifield go at it. While these guys are going at it, she noticed all the weapons they had sprawled all over

the table. It appeared to her that they were gearing up for war, so they were cleaning their weapons. There were liquor bottles on the table and weed laid beside them. The guys were clearly under the influence and weren't even paying Karly any attention. BOOM!!!!! Both the guys turned and looked the front door was wide open and Karly was gone. "Man get the hell off of me" yelled Ray "our money just went out the damn door my nigga. Fuck!!!! Yelled Mike man we have got to find her or Tony going to lay us the fuck down with no hesitation. They both go out the door behind Karly. She has no clue where the hell she is, only thing she remembers is the cabin was almost an hour drive from her party, she just couldn't remember in which direction. Ok I've got to get somewhere so I can think Karly is saying to herself, just to up and run wasn't the plan in the beginning, but it was either now or never. She spotted an abandoned house over by the water several feet ahead of her. Not knowing her exact whereabouts, and the fact that by now Mike and Ray are definitely looking for her she ran in that direction. Once reaching the abandoned house Karly quickly began looking for anything she could use to beef up her chances of survival out in the wilderness.

Yes, here's an old lantern and some matches she could see with just the little piece of moonlight seeping through the window shade. Once she lite the lantern she gasped as she turned and seen the body of Rashad's limo driver dead. Oh, shit Karly shouted loudly, if he is here then where is Rashad? Man, this shit is getting even more intense, I've been held hostage for months now with no contact cut off from all the people who love and care for me...... what am I going to do now .... Karly cried and cried. She had been through so much but couldn't seem to get herself together with all that has happened up to

now. It had been a while now since she ran from the cabin and it had started to rain, Karly searched through all the things that were in the place to find a blanket so she could at least try to get a little rest. Mike looks, it's an abandon house up ahead, you think she may have found it Ray whispered. Man, I don't fucking know, all I know is that money Tony is supposed to be bringing us is starting to fade away every moment that little bitch isn't in our grasp Mike snapped. Come on let's go see if she could have made it there responded Ray. See what happens when we try to be nice and accommodate these hoes man Ray said angrily. "It's all good brotha I have something in store for lil mama when we find her, you with it?" Mike asked. Man fuck, it why the hell not all this running this bitch has me doing, nigga you know I don't run. Once they approached the house they peaked inside through the window and noticed Karly snuggled up in front of a fire she managed to start to keep warm.

Man, I should go and just jump on that lil bitch and scare the shit out of her Ray whispered. Na man I got something better in store and we don't need that bitch all shook up before the fun gets started Mike replied. They went around the back of the house and noticed a busted window and crept inside. Once inside Mike and Ray went two separate ways, Mike went to find the breaker box to check and see if the electricity was connected in the house and Ray just stood in the hallway waiting for the queue. After about three minutes the entire house lit up, and Karly jumped straight up out of her sleep. She didn't see anyone, but she knew it had to be someone there. There was an old board with a few nails sticking out of it that she grabbed while starting to make her way through the house. As she entered the hallway Ray moved from where he was lurking and came up behind her grabbing her forcing her to

drop the board. GOTCHA BITCH Ray laughed as Karly squirmed and squiggled trying to get loose. Hold her Ray, Mike ordered hold that lil bitch still. So, this is what you do when a brotha tries to be nice and keep niggas like Ray from hurting you huh, Mike asked Karly. "It's not like that Mike, I'm grateful for you keeping me safe but I don't belong here, this has nothing to do with me" responded Karly. Oh, but it does sweetheart, you see Rashad wanted to give it all up for you lil mama and that meant all of us on his team would suffer all because this motherfucker fell in love with your little sexy ass, Ray explained. We couldn't have that, it's supposed to be

MOB (money over bitches) baby girl, and that nigga knew that said Mike. But right now, isn't the time of place to discuss that, I wanna see what the fuck got this motherfucker's panties all in a bunch, what you think Ray asked Mike? Oh, hell yes, my nigga I've been dying to find that out myself Ray responded. No please no Mike you don't have to do this, why now are you willing to hurt me Karly asked. SLAP!!! SHUT THE FUCK UP BITCH......Ray yelled. Bend your ass over hoe, Mike whispered while playing with Karly's breast. Ray positioned Karly just right over the old smelly chair while Mike held her hands down from in front of her Ray pulled off her shorts and ripped her panties. He then inserted himself in her from behind as she screamed and cried for Mike to make him stop. Please cried Karly, Mike please I'm sorry for running away.

Mike didn't give a damn about what she was saying or how she cried and yelled while Ray was having his way with her. Mike actually stood up and unfastened his belt and pulled down his zipper exposing himself to Karly as she was being taken from behind. Here bitch you wanna yell do ya, put this in your mouth and Mike forced himself in Karly's

mouth. In her mind she couldn't believe this was happening to her, but with tears in her eyes she vowed she would make them all pay. Ray then exploded all on her back and her ass, tapping Mike on his shoulder as he is having his way with Karly's mouth your turn man smiled Ray. Mike then pulled his dick out of Karly's mouth snatched her up from the chair making her stand up and bend over. Karly is gathering her thoughts thinking ok I made it I'm ok, I've had sex before just not as rough as that was, as soon as a sigh of relief crossed Karly's mind, she was forced over the arm of the chair and this time it was Mike standing behind her.

Chapter 9

He turned and looked at Ray and asked, 'how good was that pussy'', "Oh man nigga its real good' responded Ray. Well since you've had the pussy, I want what nobody's had and he spit on his hand rubbed his dick and shoved himself up in Karly's ass and took it as she screamed even more, blood started to drip down her legs. He then pulled out of that hole and went into her pussy, Karly still crying and asking him to stop, gasped for air as Mike entered her again for the second time. He was much bigger than Ray, so she really felt him as he filled up her entire hole forcibly. Feeling weak and sick to her stomach Karly tries to take it like a big girl even though the little girl inside of her is crying out for her mommy to save her. Once Mike was finished, he told her not to ever make him look like a fool again, because that is what is going to happen to her every single time, if not worse. Karly just sat in the corner crying her eyes out because she couldn't believe she just went through shit that, it reminded her of something she saw in the lifetime movies she watched. I cannot fucking believe these niggas did this to me. Mike and Ray are standing on the other side of the room laughing and joking about who made her scream and cry most. I now see why Tony referred to you motherfuckers as goons Karly said sarcastically. Oh, yea bitch well the next time you act like you got some damn sense and you won't have to go through so much pain, now go clean yourself up so we can get the fuck outta here yelled Mike. Hey Ray go with her and make sure this bitch doesn't try any more funny shit Mike ordered. I'm on it man, responded Ray. Hell, Mike, I just may get me a bit more of that thang of hers laughing Ray as he escorted Karly to the bathroom. Man, fuck all that just hurry the

77

fuck up so we can get back, you know Tony is due in tomorrow snapped Mike. As Karly is trying to make her way to the bathroom, she notices she's still dripping blood and that her walk is far from normal. She has no clue what has corresponded inside of her due to them forcibly raping her all she knows is she is in pain and it's like none she's ever felt before. Damn nigga can I go in here alone and wash my ass snapped Karly. All right girl, go ahead but leave the door cracked because if you try anything funny that's your ass......literally hahahaha laughed Ray. Karly rolled her eyes and went on in the bathroom to clean herself up. As she touched herself with the washcloth, she felt the soreness and pain ran through her lower stomach area, damn these niggas gonna pay for this shit talking to herself in the mirror, I swear on everything they going to pay for this shit she uttered. Ray a yo Ray what the fuck is taking y'all so long man we gotta go back and get the cabin right for tomorrow yelled Mike. Man, here we come Ray shouted from the top of the stairs. Karly moving slower than normal, come on girl damn you ain't hurting that bad, shit they say Rashad that nigga with the 12" dick so I know we ain't hurt that thang. Oh man shut up and let's go Mike blabbed. Making their way back through the wooded area to the cabin, the three spotted lights and stopped in their tracks. Man, I thought they were coming tomorrow, Mike, what the fuck is this Ray asked? Shit nigga I don't know, and they are supposed to be coming in tomorrow Mike reassured. Looking at one another they both utter "well who in the hell is that"? Karly looking just as surprised as they are, Mike grabs her by her hair and asked if she had called anyone while she was out on her little adventure? How the fuck could I call anyone Karly snapped while

yanking away from Mike, I do not have my phone dumbass SMACK!!! Karly falls to the ground. Damn nigga you go from protecting her to not giving a fuck about her Ray said. Man, ain't nobody playing with this bitch, and yes, I was protecting her until she made me look stupid so that shit is DONE...... said Mike. He yanks Karly up off the ground and as she is wiping the blood from her mouth, Mike whispers to her I told you I'm not a fucking toy so don't try to play with me like I'm one. Karly bites her lip and rolls her eyes at Mike. Man look Ray said shut up and look Mike.... Ray said softly. Who the hell are those dudes' man, asked Ray? Hold on, let me think I've seen that guy before Mike stated looking at the tall brown skin bother with the sharp cut. I just don't recall where I know him from Mike continued. Well, my nigga we are defenseless out in these damn woods we have got to get back in the cabin that's where all our shit is bruh barked

Ray. We can go in the back way they wouldn't even see us; I need to lay the fuck down anyways explained Karly I'm not feeling very well. Yea Mike said Ray she is right there is a way through here leading to the back of the cabin and they really wouldn't see us. Okay then point the way lil mama said Mike and don't try no sneaky shit Mike added. Karly sore and barely moving showed Mike and Ray how to get to the back of the cabin without being spotted. Once they were back in the cabin, as much as Karly hated being stuck there at that moment, she was glad to be somewhere she could take a hot bath and soothe her wounds. Go on upstairs and do whatever it is you chicks do after such an adventure chuckled Mike as Karly makes her way up the steps. She turned and looked at him and said to herself one of these days' negro...... one of these. Alright man now that we are back inside, what the fuck we going to do with these niggas outside asked Ray. For starters let's fix the

shit we knocked over fighting, at least that will make it look better in here Mike responded. While the guys were cleaning up the mess they caused while throwing their little boy tantrums a knock cam on the door. KNOCK KNOCK KNOCK...... Mike and Ray stopped in their tracks looking at one another with the look of war should it be what those visitors are looking for. Hold on one moment Ray yelled as the knocks came to the door. Mike ran over and cut on the football game as if they were watching it to begin with. Ray walks over to the door and places his hand on the doorknob but turns to Mike for the que to open the door.

Mike was sitting across the room at the kitchen table motioning for Ray to go ahead and open the door. Oh shit man what's up Ray said as he opened the door. Hey Mike, you'll never believe who it is standing here looking at me tucking his gun back in his pants. Mike gets up and walks to the door, oh shit what's up nigga Mike sounding surprised. Kevin what the hell are you doing here my nigga laughing stated Mike. Well, I'm supposed to be meeting Tony up here, Kevin responded. Oh, ok well he isn't due here until sometime tomorrow, so let's kick back, relax sip a few and reminisce Ray suggested. I can dig that homeboy, I had a long ass flight from Atlanta, and all I want is a hot shower, something to eat, a few drinks and a piece of strange ass Kevin responded. That's cool dawg we can make that happen assured Mike. Say no more than homie, where is the bathroom at I need to get out of these clothes and get comfortable Kevin asked. It's upstairs third door on the left. Man, what the fuck are you doing bruh, that's Karly's room you just sent him too Ray whispered to Mike. Yeah, I know, I just wanna see how that plays out laughed Mike. A knock comes on the door, nobody answers well I guess no one is occupying the bathroom let me get in here and get comfortable Kevin uttered to himself. Opening

80

the door flicking the light he notices he's in a bedroom and that there is someone laying on the bed. he walks around the bed and his heart begins to beat faster not knowing what to expect. He reaches for the blanket and pulls it, that's when Karly hops the hell up grabbing a piece of wood. WHOA SHAWTY!!!! Shouted Kevin. Hold on now, I thought this was the bathroom I'm sorry I didn't even know you were in the house Kevin pleaded. Figures...... Karly responded. Which one of those stupid motherfuckers gave you directions to the bathroom asked Karly? Mike.... Mike gave me directions to the bathroom said Kevin. Karly had started to lower her weapon and said, "well the bathroom is across the hall homeboy and don't bring ya ass back in here unless you want your motherfucking brains leaking, now GET OUT NIGGA!!!!!" Karly shouted. Mike and Ray heard Karly shout and came running, Mike had a stupid grin on his face since he was the one who gave Kevin the wrong directions to the bathroom. Man, calm down bitch it's not that serious, Mike shouted take your ass back to bed shit up here tripping like you done lost your mind Mike added. Karly just walked away but before closing her bedroom door she turned and looked at Mike with the most deceitful look in her eyes, which Ray caught, and he just brushed it off. Damn man that chick has went from being the quietest female I've ever known to a firecracker, maybe we should just let her go Ray bargained. SLAM!!!! Ray finds himself hitting the wall, nigga let me tell you something you fucked that bitch just like I did and now all of a sudden you are worrying about how she feels.... Yo if I get one thought that you are going soft nigga I'll kill you, Mike grinded his teeth while whispering to Ray. Pushing him away from him he headed down the stairs to finish getting ready for Tony and Nell's arrival in the morning.

Chapter 10

The cabin was finally settled for the night, Karly sat on her bed trying to wrap her head around all that has happened to her in these last few weeks. The one thing she can't help but wonder is what happened to Rashad after all these months....... Laying down trying to close her eyes she feels a sense of anger come across her. All the deceitfulness that has hit her all at once she made a vow to herself to get revenge at all costs no matter how long it takes. Every single one of these motherfuckers will pay for what they've put her and her family through, was the last thoughts on Karly's mind as she finally drifted off to sleep. KCLING LING LINGA LING all the pots and pans crash to the floor waking everybody up in the cabin even Karly. What the fuck are these idiots doing now she wonder, with no memory of dozing off the night before. DAMN NIGGA, what the fuck are you doing making all that fucking noise and shit so early in the morning Mike vented. Oh man my bad I'm just trying to at least make sure there is some breakfast cooked when Tony and Nell get her you know she's pregnant replied Ray. Damn homie I didn't know you had a bitch side in you as well Kevin teased. Both he and Mike teased Ray because he was thinking of someone else's state instead of his own. Karly, standing on the steps, overheard it all and couldn't believe what was being said. Walking back to her room she thought damn Nell's pregnant by this nigga, ain't no way of ever being cool with this bitch again. She is carrying this fools seed, of all fucking people she chooses this cornball ass nigga...... Oh well Karly thought to herself, better that bitch then me, as she began to look around her room for what she was going to wear for the day. Usually

she's in sweats and a tee, but today was different and she didn't feel like looking like the victim even though that's exactly what she was. Hey man what time is Tony due in today, Kevin asked as he started to get himself together for the day. I don't know Ray responded he only talks to Mike when he calls. Damn nigga that doesn't make you feel out of the loop when he does that, Kevin replied? Na not really to be honest with you bruh I just want my money and I'm going on about my business anyway. I could give two fucks what them niggas do all after we break bread ya feel me Ray stated. I heard that shit my nigga, maybe you should think about leaving the area, hell you could come down south with me and start all the way over hinted Kevin. Yeah man I had been thinking about that shit for a while now, Ray explained. Only thing is I wanna make sure that when I leave here, I have no reason to come the fuck back chuckled Ray. Well, shit my dude I could make a few calls and see if I can pull some strings to make that move for you a successful one my dude Kevin smiled. I can most definitely dig that big homie Ray responded. Mike steps in from outside with a puzzled look on his face as if he missed something, what y'all niggas smiling and grinning about Mike asked. Man, not a damn thing just ready for this meeting to be over so we can all go back to our normal occupations man that's all, replied Ray. Yeah, I guess it has been a long time coming, shit for a moment there I didn't think Tony was really going to come back for us my nigga stated Mike. Damn man how long has this little venture being going on man, Kevin asked? Kevin man this caper was planned over a year ago, and executed about six months ago, Ray responded. Wow it has been that long, and you haven't touched that pyt (pretty young thing) upstairs, joked Kevin. Mike and Ray paused for a moment, while Kevin glanced

back and forth at the both of them...... Well man it wasn't quite that simple, Ray confessed. Man shut up Mike yelled that bitch deserved exactly what she got...... Whoa man what the fuck are y'all niggas talking about, Kevin asked? We raped her man, and I've been feeling shitty ever since we did it, Ray confessed. See I knew you had bitch tendencies motherfucker; Mike shouted. Wait man, hold the fuck up Kevin spoke up. So y'all niggas mean to tell me that both of y'all have sampled that young pussy up there, Kevin clearified. Yelp we sure have but not the right way Ray whined. Man shut up bitch before I fuck you Mike said violently to Ray. Nigga you ain't going to do shit to me Ray shouted back. Kevin while standing in between the two calmly told them both to chill it's not that serious. We are just talking amongst men just chill. So, what Kevin you wanna test the pussy too, Mike questioned. Laughing out loud Kevin said that ass is surely phat as a motherfucker, been wondering how it looked bent over. Oh man it's even prettier bent over and those holes are so fucking tight, nigga it's as if she is still a virgin explained Mike. Damn but Rashad was hitting that right, asked Kevin. Yeah, but he only hit it once which was the night everything went down, responded Mike. In the meantime, Ray is just standing there on quiet mode listening not knowing where this conversation was going to lead. Ummm so tell me what it tastes like Mike, joked Kevin. Man, ain't nobody had time for all of that bullshit, we weren't trying to wife her just teach her ass a lesson, Ray spit out. So, I guess a nigga gotta show you goons how to go about such shit without being rough, and in return still get the pussy laughed Kevin. Kevin walked away thinking I'm going to catch this bitch coming out of the shower and tear that ass a new frame snickering entering the living room. Hmmm so what should I wear today, I wanna make myself look

84

voluptuous since Nell is all big and pregnant now, I'm going to make this bitch look stupid, Karly laughed while preparing for her shower. Dancing and prancing around her bedroom with several outfits sprawled all over the bed, damn at least I can say them stupid motherfuckers did make sure I had clothing while being held hostage she thought. Music playing softly in the background she grabs her towel and all bathing essentials and heads to the bathroom. Pulling up her hair so it doesn't get wet and looking at her face where the bruising was, she noticed it had gone down a lot. Steam is accumulating throughout the bathroom, so it was definitely time to get in the shower. Kevin made his way up the stairs hearing the shower running as he approached the top step. Oh yeah lil mama is already as I need her to be butt ass naked, he mumbled to himself. Making his way into Karly's bedroom, noticing all her clothes were laid out on the bed. Makeup sitting on the dresser, perfumes sprayed across the dresser he felt as though he just walked into a woman's clothing gallery. Preparing himself for the surprise of her life, he got comfortable in the chair by the window and waited for Karly to re-enter the room. Whoa that shower was really refreshing uttered Karly as she wrapped the towel around her dripping body. Time to brush these pearly whites girlie, shoot we got to be able to smile even in a situation as messy as this one baby, she encouraged herself. Smiling to herself in the mirror Karly exits the bathroom room and opens the door to her bedroom, drying her hair with the towel she wrapped it in. She didn't notice Kevin sitting in the chair right away. As she massaged her head, she began singing to herself, walking across the floor closing the door behind her. Like every woman who first exits the shower, and starts

85

the process of getting dressed Karly is vibing to a tune she has placed in her mind. Damn baby I knew that was something special when I first barged in on you. Karly astonished jumped....... NIGGA WHAT THE FUCK ARE YOU DOING IN MY ROOM? Karly shouted while wrapping her towel tightly around her figure eight built body. Chill baby girl chill it ain't like that, if I were going to take something I'd did that while you were grooving your way through the room., responded Kevin. I just wanted to talk to you girl, maybe you can help me he explained. I need to know what happened to my baby brother Rashad...... Karly's heart dropped to her feet as she stood astonished by what just came out of Kevin's mouth. Karly stood with her mouth wide opened still at a loss for words. Listen sit down we don't have much time, explained Kevin. Them katz down there actually believe I was coming up here to take the pussy, so after a while they are going to have to hear some kind of noise or both our asses will end up in the ground, you got me he asked Karly. Look I don't know what the hell you got going on, but my baby didn't have any siblings, hell he didn't even know his real parents snapped Karly as she started to put on her clothes while the towel was wrapped around her. I don't believe a damn thing you're saying Karly went on. For all I know your just like all the rest of them niggas, she explained. I don't trust nobody anymore, everybody I thought was down with me turned out to be jealous and envies, so what the hell makes you any different? Kevin went to the door and peaked out to make sure nobody was coming, and he reached in his back pocket, pulling out his wallet and a newspaper clipping. The paper read "MOBSTER AND FAMILY SLAUGHTERED, TWO KIDS MISSING". See my brother and I were at out basketball game that night

and when we arrived home, there were cops and ambulances everywhere. There as we walked up to the house stood a dude, we had seen plenty of times whom we called Big Tone. I guess you could call him our father's right-hand man. He was always at our house with pop whether it was to help around the house or to take us wherever we wanted to go Big Tone was there. Kevin sat in a daze; hey Karly shook him to bring him back around. Are you telling me that you and Rashad's father was a mobster, Karly asked? Yeah, one of the biggest of all time Kevin answered. Our mother was a schoolteacher so when it came to our education, she handled that. So how did you guys get split up Karly asked? Shh shh listen here comes the guys, when I tell you to start moaning as if we're fucking and I'll bounce on the bed whispered Kevin. Karly shook her head, and as Mike and Ray approached the bedroom, they heard her moaning and groaning and the bed bouncing. Damn it sounds like that bitch just willingly gave the pussy up to that pretty motherfucker, mumbled Mike. Man come on let's finish getting this house done before Tony gets here. Damn, alright man let's get this shit done, I'm ready to get back to my grind anyway shit, Mike gritted. Turning to go back downstairs Kevin peeps out the door and motions to Karly to stop the moaning and groaning noise. The two them had managed to pull a fast one over on the goons and were safe for now. Shit, that was close whispered Karly we have got to figure out something and really fast because Tony is due like any moment negro Karly assured. Well, I'm going to have to sell this shit so come here Kevin ordered Karly. Hell, no nigga you better figure out a way to sell it without me, she snapped. Shoving her up against the closet, Kevin stuck his hands down Karly's pants as she squirmed trying to pull away, she knew the way he had her she would possibly hurt herself.

So, standing there until he was finished doing whatever it was, he was doing would be the safest unharmful thing she could do at that moment. After about three minutes he began to pull his hand from her pants looking her in her eyes, he placed his fingers in his mouth and smiled. Turning and exiting her room, Karly mumbled these niggas need to be taught a lesson slamming her door behind him. Damn what am I going to do she thought. How do I know this kat is really Rashad's brother, never mind that where the hell has, he been all these years Karly wondered? Sitting there with so many different thoughts in her head she almost forgot

Tony and Chanelle were due to arrive at the cabin shortly. She pulled her hair up and put on a few touches of makeup to seem as if she's adapted to being held hostage. Karly was always the one out of her and Chanelle who didn't mind a scuffle, so the hard role wasn't hard for her to maintain. As she slid her high-top Nike's on her feet making sure they are lessened up tight enough in case she had to run it wouldn't be a struggle. Putting on a tank top with a short sleeve Nike shirt to match her shoes, Karly was determined to be comfortable and was dressed for any occasion at that moment. Standing in the mirror she prayed to the lord that he brings her out of this mess and with wisdom, knowledge, as well as understanding. Looking around for her bookbag she began to place some extra things in there she may need should she get away up out of there. Taking a deep breathe she opened the bedroom door just in time to hear the dudes downstairs greeting Tony and Chanelle. Kissing the cross she wore around her neck she began down the stairs, leaving her bag in the door of the bedroom out of sight. As she made her way down the stairs Tony notices, she has gained a few pounds and how cute she

still is, whereas Chanelle had gotten big and out of shape due to the baby she was carrying. Damn girl I see you still fine as hell, even when being held hostage huh, Tony smiled. Whatever Karly responded rolling her eyes. You look marvelous Chanelle, Karly said looking at Chanelle. Oh yeah, girl please you know darn well I look like a damn whale with a penguin wobble snapped Chanelle. Karly smirked and said Well I think it's cute on you Nelle while walking towards the dining table. Man, I wonder what it is these guys have on their minds Karly thought to herself. Everything is going smoothly right now; something isn't right with this vibe. Karly glances over the entire room and how everyone in the room was placed. It almost seemed like the plan was unfolding right before her eyes. She closed her eyes and began to silently pray asking God to shield her from whatever seemed to be coming her way. She didn't know what exactly what that was, but she could feel something wasn't right. Hey Karly, can we talk Chanelle asked, sure why not all I've had is time here lately Karly stated nonchalantly. Listen you need to get out of here, tony doesn't plan to give either of those guys any money, Chanelle whispered. He only came here to tie up loose ends Karly, Chanelle assured. What panicked Karly, shhhh Chanelle whispered. Karly, you have got to get out of here, you shouldn't have gotten tied up in all of this and I'm so very sorry I truly am, Chanelle cried. Oh my god Nelle, calm down getting upset isn't good for the baby, Karly mentioned. Karly it's so much I want to tell you but now isn't the time, you're not a dumb chick just get out of here boo it's not going to end well for you if you stay, said Chanelle. Karly got up and headed back up the stairs, she had a bag up there with enough stuff to keep her warm and moving for at least two days, or until she can get to civilization. She knew she didn't have much time to put a plan together, so it was either now or never. She closed the bedroom door quietly. Praying to the lord above as she opened the window and threw out her Nike bag. She's on the second floor so she knows when she maneuver's herself to let go she will have to brace herself. Father in the name of Jesus please cover me as I step into this journey back to my old life, in Jesus' name I pray Amen....... Karly said as she let go of the window. THUMP... lord that was easier than I thought sighed Karly. Brushing herself off, she grabbed her bag and started towards the woods. Karly didn't want to leave Chanelle, but at this moment only the lord could save her. Man, I really hate to leave my girl like this, but I have got to get the hell out of here before these dudes kill me, Karly stated while making her way through the woods. Hey Tony, are you ready for the baby to get here man, asked Ray. Man, I'm not here for all that small talk nigga, I'm only here to settle this doubt once and for all snapped Tony. Hey girl bring me that bag I sat beside the door Tony snapped at Chanelle. Damn nigga that girl carrying your baby and you want her to go get that heavy ass bag, even I have compassion at times my nigga said Mike. Ha ha ha ha ha laughed Tony, nigga you got a lot of mouth, so I guess I'll give you yours first and get you on out the way he continued. Looking around he noticed Chanelle slowly moving back to the chair to sit down but didn't see Karly anywhere. A nigga WHERE THE GIRL AT, YELLED TONY....... Oh man calm the hell down she hasn't went anywhere but back up to her room, she does that a lot when she isn't up for conversating, explained Ray. Look check it, I'll go up and get her so you can go ahead and break us off and we all can go our separate ways

90

sighed Kevin as he headed towards the stairs. Come on Tony let us see that loot my dude, Mike replied. Damn near upstairs Kevin realized Karly's room was quiet and could feel a bit of a draft coming from it. Oh, shit baby girl I really hope you haven't done what it's starting to seem like you did, mumbled Kevin. Approaching her room his suspicion is confirmed Karly was gone. SHIT SHIT SHIT SHIT as he smacked his forehead, knowing this has now opened the door to a whole other ordeal. Bracing himself as he started back down the stairs, with what seemed like a million different thoughts going through his mind all of which ending with Karly being killed. TONY...... MAN SHE GONE!!!!! Tony looked at Mike and Ray pulled his 9mm and emptied the clip between the two. CLASH, the front door comes off the hinges, BOSS YOU GOOD, yells the four men who stepped through the door with their guns drawn. Yeah, assures Tony, take this nigga Kevin and go into the woods and find that bitch he ordered she knows way too much. Consider it done spoken from the biggest nigga of the four. When we find her what do you want done to her, asked one of the other guys. Tony looked over at Chanelle, do whatever you feel she deserves, but don't kill her just make her wish she were dead, replied to Tony. Ok we'll be checking in with you, as soon as we come up with the route she took.

Chapter 11

Just a few miles to go and I should be out of these woods, Karly said as she crossed over a little bridge. I wonder her Chanelle is doing, lord please continue to keep your hands on her. While you at its Jesus can you please show me some sign that Rashad is still alive. Looking around she decided she would sit down and take a break. It had been about 45 minutes to an hour since she got away from the cabin. If they haven't noticed by now that I'm gone then I have a good enough start, she thought to herself. Chanelle, how you feeling baby Tony asked as he took a sit and pulled it up in front of her. I'm ok Tony, baby kicking as usual but I'm ok Chanelle responded shockingly. Tony hadn't asked her in months how she or the baby was feeling so she knew something was up. Chanelle I'm wondering what you and Karly spoke about while the boys and I were conducting business in the other room, Tony explained. Oh well she did not say much just told me how cute I was pregnant, you know things girls talk about honey, Chanelle spoke quietly. Tony got up and walked around Chanelle and rubbing and kissing on her, damn baby you seem tense are you sure everything is ok, he said. Rubbing her neck, he then began to squeeze it tightly while whispering in her ear, I know you have something to do with her running away, and to think I chose your ass over her fine ass he said. It is ok you too shall get what you deserve wrapping his arm around her neck choking her and then breaking her neck. Chanelle's body went limp. Tony grabbed his duffle bag and Mike and Ray's guns from their pants and walked out the cabin. Tony went out to the trunk of the car her was in and grabbed a gasoline can. Going back in the

house he poured gas all around the house only to lead it right back outside. Having then pulled a zippo lighter from his pocket, lit it and through it into the house. Standing there as he watched the house burn and burn fast. Karly waking up from her power nap she got up and noticed a dim light flickering through the woods in the direction of the cabin. Her breathing started to get heavy, not knowing what has happened she took off in the opposite direction with what seemed like a million thoughts running through her mind. Calm down Karly, she began to talk to herself. You are going to make it out of here just calm down. Picking her their pace the bodyguards of Tony are covering much ground. Damn how much more forest is it out here, mumbled one of the men. The leader responded it's enough, but she can't be too far ahead of us we'll get her. Well G what are we going to do to her when we find her, asked one guy. Kevin just walking looking, all while praying and hoping they don't find Karly. Hey young blood, you've been quiet since we left the cabin what's up with that the older guard asked

Kevin? Man, it's nothing up just ready to get this shit done and over with man that's all responded Kevin. Shhh, everybody stops where you are, whispered the man in the front. She's not far from here at all I smell her perfume. Damn Kevin tapped one of the guards and asked how the hell did he do that. Oh, that's Duke, he's a retired seal. Oh, damn my girl isn't making it out of this shit at all he thought to himself. POW POW POW POW, they started firing into the woods. What was that Kevin asked? My fault I thought I heard something, man he said not to kill her, Kevin snapped. Wait hold up blood you sure you with us, because the last nigga who tried to save a damsel in distress got cancelled my dawg mentioned Duke. Whatever I was just reminding y'all that's all.

Stopping trying to catch her breath Karly heard those shots fired into the woods and two ripped through her shoulder and leg. She's been hit and it hurt but she was determined to keep it moving. She made it through all the abuse for the past several months, she knew she was going to make it out of this as well. She saw a little cave like area about 50 meters from where she was. Thinking to herself if I can just make it in there, I know I will be able to hold up there for a bit. Not knowing how many guys Tony has sent after her, Karly must get to that cave like area and hide out for as long as she can. God if I can just make it out of this, I will forever praise you for all you've done and how you've kept me from dangers seen and unseen, Karly uttered while looking up to the night's sky. Moving slowly but quickly trying not to make too much noise giving her location up to the guys who are tracking her. She moved as swiftly but as gentle as she possibly could being wounded. Hey.... hold up, I thought I seen something moving over that way. They all shifted to their left, there was a crackle in the woods, but not a loud enough one for it to be her. It was too lite of a crackle Duke said. Thank you, Jesus, Karly sighed as she reached the cave like area. Looking around she wanted to make sure there weren't any wild animals like wolves, deer, bores or things of that nature inside before she went in. Once inside, Karly sat down as slowly as she could to keep the pain from being intense. Looking in her bag for something she could use for a bandage to slow down the bleeding in her leg and shoulder. She used a long sleeve shirt ripping it into two separate pieces to bandage her wounds. She needed to rest, to give body a chance to regain some of its strength, since so much of it has gone due to the wounds she sustained. I'll stay here until the sun comes up, at least then I have a chance of getting out of these woods for good.

94

One of the guys walked a few more steps and realized there was a cave like figure far off and wondered if they should check it out. Hey, look over there, the guy shouted. Do you guys see that, I bet you she is right inside hiding out he joked. Man stops playing around, it's getting later, and later Duke mentioned. She wouldn't be dumb enough to hide in such an obvious area. They all shrugged it off and kept going passing the cave like figure. About a mile after seeing the cave they all decided to split up in two groups, figuring they could cover more area with two groups instead of being in just one. So, as they separated, Kevin couldn't help but wonder if Karly was in that cave hiding. He wanted to check to check but knew he couldn't do so without getting himself killed as well as her. He needed a plan, looking at the guy he was paired with he knew he'd have to kill him in order to go back and check the cave. Kevin then out a plan in motion, he would lead the guy far enough away from the cave and the other group of guys and kill him. Thing was how could he kill him without shooting so the others wouldn't hear the gun? So, as they walked Kevin looked around trying to see if he could find something to beat the guy with, so he could go check out the cave without telling Karly's whereabouts if she is in the cave. Tripping and falling over a log, the guy turned around to see if Kevin was ok extending out his hand. As he reached for Kevin's hand to help him up, Kevin pulled him down to the ground with him. As the two wrestles on the ground Kevin managed to get his hand on a tree branch and hit the other guy over the head rendering him unconscious. DAMN!!!! That little dude took some wind out of me, Kevin gasped. Heading back to the cave he noticed the other guys were already in the area of the cave, so he had to squat down behind a tree

to watch what they were doing. A Duke, are you sure you don't want me to look into that cave sir, asked the youngest guy? I would hate for us to bypass that cave and it turned out later on she was in there the entire time, mentioned the youngest guy. You know what fine, snapped Duke check the damn cave boy GO NOW!!!!! The guy gets closer to the cave and Kevin sees him, so he picked up something and through it across the cave to another area, which grabbed their attention. So, he didn't get a chance to venture on into the cave. OH SHIT, Karly said as she heard the commotion outside the cave. She peeped out and realized the guys were right outside and with her wounds she knew she couldn't outrun either of them. Oh my gosh, what am I going to do this time, she begins to cry and mumble. Hey Karly, are you in there, whispered Kevin. It's me Kevin, are you there he asked again. Yes, Kevin I'm here, what are you doing here, she said. Can I come in, he asked? Yea hurry up before they see you, Karly responded. Kevin entered in the cave and once he got closer to Karly, he realized she was injured. We've got to get you out of here baby girl, Kevin whispered. I'll carry you out of these woods, and I'll make up something, but I need you to find my brother for me. Can you promise me that Karly, asked Kevin? Yes, Karly answered, I will definitely find Rashad and I'll let him know you're one the reasons I made it out of here alive. Kevin helped Karly gather her things and they left out of the cave before the other three guys doubled back to check the cave. Kevin started off walking with Karly on his back. When he heard the guys coming, he started to pick up the pace. Duke, there she goes, and someone is carrying her, mentioned the little guy. Shoot them, shoot them both Duke ordered. But man....... NIGGA I SAID

SHOOT THEM BOTH, Duke yelled. The other two guys opened fire. Missing the two several times, GIVE ME

YOUR GUN AND ILL SHOW YOU HOW TO KILL A MOTHERFUCKER, Duke snapped. Boss you're forgetting what tony said, one of the guys reminding Duke of his orders. Duke pointed the gun in his direction and asked him if he wanted to continue to be a part of this world? If you don't bring up tony and the instructions he originally asked for and you'll be going to meet your maker tonight young nigga, said Duke. Kevin slowed down running once he felt as though he left those guys, I knew that nigga Kevin was a snake and had a connection with the girl from the moment he opened his mouth. That's cool though, you got your phone young nigga. Yes, sir I have it, responded the young boy. Give it here snapped Duke, he got on the phone and called Tony. Hey boss man Duke started, the girl had help. That nigga Kevin helped her get away from us. Oh, ok that's what I wanted to know, I'll holla at you in a bit, peace Duke passed the phone back. What he wants us to do Boss, asked the young boy. Kill both of them but torture them first, responded Duke. Listen if that nigga Kevin with her, where is slim? Man, you know that nigga had to have killed him in order to get away and get to the girl, barked the other guy. Let's go get the car, because when they get out of the woods, they are going to be on the highway uttered Duke. Once they hit that highway it is going to be harder to track them. We going to cut him off in their tracks, they got about two hours before they get to the highway, we will be there waiting for them when they do, Duke assured. Heading back towards the cabin the guys could not help but wonder where their other guy was and why did not Duke go looking for him. Walking back to the cabin was done at a steady pace but incredibly quiet between the three guys. Hey baby girl you ok, asked Kevin? No, I feel so crappy, I know that bastard killed Nelle, I

just know he did, smirked Karly. Yes, well we must get you away from this area before your next, responded Kevin. Oh, I am making it out of this because it is a lot of unanswered questions that I personally need the answers too snapped Karly. I do not understand how someone could be so cruel, and even harm someone who treated him like a brother she ranted. I do not get it, and someone owes me so serious answers Kevin, she continued. One way or another I will get them, and I do not care who tries to stop me, as long as God gives me strength, someone is going to tell me what's going on, Karly assured Kevin. Well baby girl makes sure you be careful because I believe it's bigger than all of this mess, Kevin stated. It must be for everything to go like it has this past several months. Besides if it were low life people who illustrated this plot to begin with Karly, you would have been dead love, Kevin said. Wait hold up what is that I hear, Karly asked?........ Oh my God Kevin it sounds like the highway, surprisingly Karly said. Well damn, that was easier than I thought it would be, Kevin proceeded. Baby girl do you think you can walk a bit, you got my back a little sore, Kevin whined. Oh boy shut up, I am not even all that big Karly teased and laughed. Let me down boy, since your back hurts so much, she said while chuckling. Kevin stopped and let Karly down easily they both laughed and joked. I am glad through all this foolishness we can laugh, and joke Kevin said. Damn right, all that we've both endured, you are losing your brother and me losing my best friend and lover. It feels good to laugh, said Karly. Both begin to walk through the last part of the woods, crossing over a bridge which had a pond flowing underneath. Come on girl, we are almost to the finish line, teased Kevin. Ahahahahahah Kevin laughed

when suddenly, his laugh goes mute, and he begins to fall. Come on boy what is wrong with you,

KEVIN!!!!!KEVIN!!!!!KEVIN!!!!!! you are scaring me girl, Kevin hollered. As he fell as a limp as a noodle, she noticed blood on her hands from holding him around his waist. Oh my god, you have been shot Karly screamed. She panicked not knowing where the bullet came from, trying to stay low and scope out the surrounding area he is scared and do not know what to do. She tries to pull Kevin to safety not knowing what is going to happen next, all she knows is someone is trying to pick her off and she doesn't stand a chance if she doesn't take cover. Karly looked down at Kevin who didn't possess a sign of life left in him, so she laid him down and ran for cover. Carefully choosing a secure hiding spot since he didn't know who, what, when, where how or why at this present moment he had to be careful. After hiding for a while, she heard steps coming from across the bridge. Peeping out from behind the tree she seen the other guys who were tracking her and then she seen Tony. He motioned for the guys to pick him up and toss his body in the river below the bridge. Karly remained out of sight as she watched them throw Kevin's motionless body over the bridge. Watching him fall into the water and the current take him away just broke her heart. As she got up to finish making her way across the bridge out of the woods to the highway, she noticed the cars and truck were gone. This meant the coast was clear, and at least one of them can still take the journey to finding out what happened to Rashad. Approaching the highway she heard a horn blow, turning towards the horn she heard POP.... POP.... POP...., Karly realizing she got hit held her stomach applying pressure, walked a few more steps before collapsing on side of the highway.......... Hey, hey Ms can you hear me.......

Made in the USA
Middletown, DE
07 March 2025